No Holly
for
Miss Quinn

Also by Miss Read

Village School

Village Diary

Storm in the Village

Thrush Green

Fresh from the Country

Winter in Thrush Green

Miss Clare Remembers

Over the Gate

Village Christmas

The Market Square

The Howards of Caxley

The Fairacre Festival

News from Thrush Green

Emily Davis

Tyler's Row

The Christmas Mouse

Farther Afield

Battles at Thrush Green

No Holly
for
Miss Quinn

MISS READ

With Drawings by J. S. Goodall

Houghton Mifflin Company Boston
1976

Library of Congress Cataloging in Publication Data

Read, Miss.
  No holly for Miss Quinn.

  I. Title.
PZ4.S132No3   [PR6069.A42]   823'.9'14   76–17327
ISBN 0–395–24768–3

Printed in the United States of America

c 10 9 8 7 6 5 4 3 2 1

TO

Betty and Alan

WITH LOVE

CONTENTS

No Holly
for
Miss Quinn

HOLLY LODGE

*I*F YOU TAKE the road from the downland village of Fairacre to Beech Green, you will notice three things.

First, it is extremely pretty, with flower-studded banks or wide grass verges, clumps of trees, and a goodly amount of hawthorn hedging.

Second, it runs steadily downhill, which is not surprising as the valley of the river Cax lies about six miles southward.

Third, it loops and curls upon itself in the most snake-like manner, so that if you are driving it is necessary to negotiate the bends prudently, in third gear, and with all senses alert.

Because of the nature of the road, then, a certain attractive house, set back behind a high holly hedge, escapes the attention of the passer-by.

Holly Lodge began modestly enough as a small cottage belonging to a farming family at Beech Green. No one knows the name of the builder, but it would have been some local man who used the materials to hand, the flints from the earth, the oak from the woods, and straw from the harvest fields, to fashion walls, beams, and thatched roof. When the work was done, he chipped the date "1773" on the king beam, collected his dues, and went on to the next job.

It is interesting to note that the first occupant of the cottage when preparing for Christmas in that year would be unaware of the exciting events happening on the other side of the Atlantic, which would have such influence upon the lives of his children, and those who would follow them, as tenants of the farmer. The Boston Tea Party would mean nothing to him, as he brought in his Christmas logs for the hearth. But a hundred and seventy years later, Americans would live under that thatched roof, in time of war, and be welcomed by the villagers of Fairacre.

By that time, the modest two-up-and-two-down cottage had been enlarged so that there were three bedrooms and a bathroom upstairs, and a large kitchen below. The lean-to of earlier days, which had housed the washtub, the strings of onions, and the dried bunches of herbs for winter seasoning, had vanished. Despite war-time stringencies, the house was cared for and the garden trim, and the owner, John Phipps, serving with his regiment, longed for the day of his return.

It never came. He was killed in the Normandy landings on D-day, and the house was sold. It changed hands several times, and, partly because of this and partly because of its retired position, about a mile from the center of Fairacre, Holly Lodge always seemed secret and aloof. The people who took it were always "outsiders," retired worthies from Caxley in the main, with grown-up families and a desire for a quiet life in a house small enough to be manageable without domestic help.

The last couple to arrive, some two hundred years after the builder had carved his date on the king beam, were named Benson. Ambrose Benson was a retired bank manager from Caxley and his wife Joan, once a school mistress, was a bustling sixty-year-old. Their only son was up at Cambridge, their only daughter married with three children.

Fairacre, as always, was interested to see the preparations being made before the couple moved in. The holly hedge, unfortunately, screened much activity, and the fact that Holly Lodge was some distance from the village itself dampened the usual ardor of the gossip hunters. Nevertheless, it was soon learned that an annex was being built at one end of the house, comprising a sitting room, bedroom, bathroom, and kitchen, which would be occupied by Mrs. Benson's elderly mother.

Mr. Willet, caretaker at Fairacre School, sexton of

St. Patrick's, and general handyman to the whole
village, was the main source of such snippets of news
about Holly Lodge as were available. The builder of
the annex, although a Caxley man, was a distant
cousin of Mrs. Willet's, and asked if her husband
could give a hand laying a brick path round the new
addition.

It was a job after Mr. Willet's heart. He enjoyed
handling the old rosy bricks, matching them for
color, aligning them squarely, and making a lasting
object of beauty and use. All his spare time, in the
month before the Bensons were due to take over, he

spent in their garden at his task, humming to himself as he worked.

His happiness was marred only by his impatience with the dilatory and slapdash ways of the builders.

"To see them sittin' on their haunches suppin' tea," said Mr. Willet to his friend Mr. Lamb, the postmaster at Fairacre, "fair makes my blood boil. And that fathead of a plumber has left the new bath standing in the middle of the lawn so that there's a great yellow mark where the grass has been killed."

"Marvelous, ennit!" agreed Mr. Lamb. "D'you reckon they'll get in on time?"

"Not the way those chaps are carrying on," snorted Mr. Willet. "Be lucky to get in by Christmas, if you ask me."

Mr. Willet's contribution to the amenities of Holly Lodge was finished before the end of August. The Bensons had hoped to be in residence by then but, as Mr. Willet had forecast, they had to await the departure of the plasterer, the painters, and the plumber.

At last, on a mercifully fine October day, the removal vans rolled up, and Fairacre had the pleasure of knowing that the newcomers had really arrived.

Joan Benson was soon studied, discussed, and finally approved by the village. She was a plump bird-like little woman, quick in speech and movement, given to wearing pastel colors and rather more jewelry than Fairacre was used to. Nevertheless,

she was outstandingly friendly. She joined the
Women's Institute and made a good impression by
offering to help with the washing up, a task which
the local gentry tended to ignore.

Even Mrs. Pringle, the village's arch-moaner, had
to admit that "she'd settled in quite nice for a town
woman," but could not resist adding that Time-
Alone-Would-Tell. Ambrose Benson was not much
seen in the village, but it was observed that the garden at Holly Lodge was being put into good shape
after the ravages of the builders' sojourn, and that he
seemed to be enjoying his retirement in the new
home.

Mr. Partridge, the vicar of Fairacre, had called
upon his new parishioners and had high hopes of per-
suading Ambrose Benson to take part in the nu-
merous village activities which needed just such a
person as a retired bank manager to see to them.
How Fairacre had managed to muddle along before
his arrival, Ambrose began to wonder, as he listened
to the good vicar's account of the pressing needs of
various committees, but, naturally, he kept this
thought to himself.

"A charming fellow," Gerald Partridge told his
wife. "I'm sure he will be a great asset to Fairacre."

The third member of the household was rarely
seen. Joan's mother was eighty-seven, smitten with
arthritis, and had difficulty in getting about. But the

villagers agreed that she did the most beautiful knitting, despite her swollen fingers, and smiled very sweetly from the car when her daughter took her for a drive.

When the Bensons' first Christmas at Holly Lodge arrived, it was generally agreed in Fairacre that the vicar might be right.

Ambrose Benson, his wife, and mother-in-law could well prove to be an asset to the village.

The winter was long and hard. It was not surprising that little was seen of the newcomers. Holly Lodge, snug behind the high hedge which gave it its name, seemed to be in a state of hibernation. Joan Benson was seen occasionally in the Post Office or village shop, but Ambrose, it seemed, tended to have bronchial trouble and did not venture far in icy weather. As for old Mrs. Penwood, her arthritis made it difficult to get from one room to the other, and she spent more and more time in the relative comfort of a warm bed.

"I shall be extra glad to see the spring," admitted Joan to Mr. Lamb, as she posted a parcel to her daughter. "My husband and mother are virtually housebound in this bitter weather. I long to get out into the garden, and I know they do too."

"Won't be long now," comforted Mr. Lamb, looking at the bleak village street through the window.

But Mr. Lamb was wrong. Bob Willet, weather prophet among his many other roles, was stern in his predictions.

"We won't get no warmth till gone Easter," he told those who asked his opinion. "Then we'll be lucky. Might well be Whitsun afore it picks up."

"Ain't you a Job's comforter, eh?" chaffed one listener. But he secretly respected Bob Willet's forecasts. Too often he was right.

On one of the darkest days of January, when a gray lowering sky gave the feeling of being in a tent and Fairacre folk were glad to draw the blinds at four o'clock against such an inhospitable world, news went round the village grape vine that poor Ambrose Benson had been taken by ambulance to Caxley Hospital.

"Couldn't hardly draw breath," announced Mrs. Pringle, who had received the news via Minnie Pringle, her niece, who had had it from the milkman. "Choking his life out, he was. I've always said that anything attacking the bronichals is proper cruel. It was congested bronichals that carried off my Uncle Albert, and him only fifty-two."

The next day, the Bensons' daughter arrived, and the following day their son.

Gerald Partridge, the vicar, calling to offer sympathy and help, found the two ladies at Holly Lodge red-eyed but calm.

"He is putting up a marvelous fight, they tell me," said Joan Benson, "and he has always been very fit, apart from this chest weakness. We are full of hope."

"If there is anything I, or my wife, can do, please call upon us," begged the vicar. "You are all very much in our thoughts, and we shall pray for your husband's recovery on Sunday morning."

"You are so kind. We've been quite overwhelmed with sympathetic enquiries. Really, Fairacre is the friendliest place, particularly when trouble has struck."

True to his word, Mr. Partridge and his congregation prayed earnestly for Ambrose's restoration to health. But, even as they prayed, the sick man's life was ebbing, and by the time the good people emerged into St. Patrick's wintry churchyard, Ambrose Benson had drawn his last painful breath.

This tragic blow, coming at the end of a long spell of anxiety, hit Joan cruelly. For years, she and Ambrose had looked forward to his retirement. They had planned trips abroad, holidays in London where they could satisfy their love for the theater, and, of course, the shared joys of the new home and its garden. Now all was shattered.

In a daze, she dealt with the dismal arrangements for the funeral, thankful to have her son and daughter with her over the first dreadful week of widowhood.

Luckily, Ambrose's affairs had been left in apple-pie order, as was to be expected from a methodical bank manager, but it was plain that Joan would need to be careful with money in the years ahead.

When her son and daughter departed, after the funeral, Joan was thankful to have the company of her mother in the house. The old lady seemed frailer than ever, and Joan took to sleeping in the spare bed put up in her mother's room.

The annex had been planned on one floor, and during those nights when Joan lay awake, listening to the shallow breathing of her mother and the queer little whimpers which she sometimes made unconsciously as the arthritis troubled her dreams, she began to appreciate the charm of the new addition to Holly Lodge.

Sometimes she wondered if she might let it, and install her mother on the ground floor of the main house. Many a night was passed in planning rooms and arranging furniture, and this helped a little in mitigating the dreadful waves of grief which still engulfed her.

It was during this sad time that Joan found several true friends in Fairacre. Mrs. Partridge and Mrs.

Mawne were particularly understanding, visiting frequently, and taking it in turns to sit with Mrs. Penwood so that Joan could have a brief shopping expedition to Caxley or a visit to old friends in the town.

She was met with sympathy and kindness wherever she went in the village, and became more and more determined to remain at Holly Lodge as, she felt sure, Ambrose would have wished.

Spring was late in arriving, as Bob Willet had forecast, and it was late in April that the first really warm day came.

"I shall sit out," said Mrs. Penwood decidedly. "Put my chair in the shelter of the porch, Joan, and I will enjoy the fresh air after all these months of being a prisoner."

"It is still quite chilly," said Joan. "Do you think it is wise?"

"Of course it's wise!" responded her mother. "It will do me more good than all the doctor's pills put together."

With difficulty, Joan settled her mother in the sunshine. She was swathed in a warm cloak and had a mohair rug over her legs, but Joan was alarmed to find how cold her hands were when she took her some coffee.

Mrs. Penwood brushed aside her daughter's protestations.

"I haven't been so happy since Ambrose —" she began, and hastily changed this to, "for months. The air is wonderful. Just what I need."

She insisted on having her light lunch outside, and Joan watched her struggling to hold a spoon with numbed fingers.

"Do come inside after lunch, Mother," she begged. "You've really had the best of the day, you know."

But the old lady was adamant. In some ways, thought Joan, as she washed up, it was far simpler to cope with half a dozen children. At least they recognized authority, even if they did not always obey it. Old ladies, however sweet-natured, did not see why they should take orders from those younger than themselves.

She returned to find her mother sleeping, and decided to let her have another half an hour before she insisted on moving her indoors. Carefully, she spread another rug over the sleeping form, tucking the cold hands beneath it. Already the air was beginning to cool, and Joan went in to light the fire, ready for a cheerful tea-time.

A few minutes later, she heard cries and groans from her mother, and hurried outside. The old lady appeared to be having a spasm, and made incoherent noises. The only word which Joan could understand was the anguished cry of "Pain, pain!"

Fear gave her strength to wrest the old lady, coverings and all, from the chair and to stumble with her to the bedroom in the annex. Swiftly she managed to put her, still fully clothed, into bed, and ran to the telephone.

Their old family doctor from Caxley arrived within the hour, examined his patient minutely, and shook his head.

"I shall give her an injection now," he told Joan. "Just see that she remains warm and quiet. I will look in again after this evening's surgery."

Joan nodded, too stricken to speak.

"Got a good neighbor handy to keep you company?" asked the doctor, knowing how recently she had been widowed.

"I will telephone the vicar's wife," whispered Joan.

"I'll do it for you," said the doctor.

Within five minutes, Mrs. Partridge arrived, and the doctor went to his car.

"I'm afraid Mrs. Penwood is in a pretty poor way," he confided to the vicar's wife as she saw him off. "It's a sad task to leave you with, but I will be back soon after seven."

He was as good as his word. But when Mrs. Partridge opened the door of Holly Lodge to him, he saw at once that his patient had gone.

❦

Joan Benson spent that night, and the next one, at the vicarage, and the bonds formed then between the two women were to remain strong throughout their lives.

After this second blow, Joan went to stay for a time with her daughter. The children's chatter, and their need of her, gave her comfort, and she had time to try to put her plans in order.

She decided to stay. Holly Lodge might seem rather large for one widowed lady, but her children and grandchildren would need bedrooms when they visited, and she did not want to part with much-loved possessions.

But the annex, she decided, must be let. It was

quite self-contained, and would make a charming home for some quiet woman in circumstances such as her own, or for that matter, for a mature woman with a job.

The Caxley Chronicle carried an advertisement in early June. Several people came to see Joan Benson but nobody seemed really suitable.

It was Henry Mawne, the vicar's friend and a distinguished ornithologist, who first mentioned Miss Quinn.

"She's secretary to my old friend Barney Hatch in Caxley," he told Joan. "I know she needs somewhere. Her present digs are noisy, and she likes a quiet life. Nice woman, thirtyish, keeps old Barney straight, and that takes some doing. Like me to mention it?"

"Yes, please. I would be grateful."

And thus it came about that Miriam Quinn, personal private secretary to Sir Barnabas Hatch, the financier, came to look at Holly Lodge's annex one warm June evening, breathed in the mingled scent of roses and pinks, and surveyed the high hedge which ensured privacy, with the greatest satisfaction.

"I should like to come very much," she said gravely to Joan Benson.

"And I," said that lady joyfully, "should like you to. Shall we go inside and settle things?"

Chapter 2

MISS QUINN ARRIVES

M ISS QUINN MOVED IN on a still cloudless day in July. Fairacre was looking its best, as all downland country does, in summer heat.

Wild roses and honeysuckle embroidered the hedges. The cattle stood in the shade of the trees, swishing away the flies with their tails and chewing the cud languorously. Dragonflies skimmed the surface of the diminishing river Cax, and a field of beans in flower wafted great waves of scent through the car's open window as Miss Quinn trundled happily towards her new home.

Before her the road shimmered in the heat. It was almost a relief to enter the shady tunnel of trees at Beech Green, before regaining the open fields which led to Fairacre at the foot of the downs.

Her spirits rose as she left Caxley behind. Miriam Quinn had been brought up in a vicarage in a lonely stretch of the fen country. Space and solitude were the two things which that windswept area had made essential to her happiness. Sometimes she longed for the great Cambridge sky when the canyons of some city streets drove her near to claustrophobic panic, and even the pleasant tree-lined road in Caxley, where she had lived since taking up the post with Sir Barnabas, she found stuffy and oppressive.

Now she would live in open country again. The encircling holly hedge, which gave her new abode its name, would not worry her. The windows of the annex, she had noticed swiftly, looked mainly upon the flank of the downs. She reckoned that she could see seven or eight miles to the distant woods to the south of Caxley from her sitting room window.

She reached the signpost saying FAIRACRE 1, and began to look out for the hidden drive on her left which ran beside the high holly hedge to the main gate of Holly Lodge. It was propped open ready for her, she was grateful to see, and her own garage had its door hospitably open.

Miriam Quinn shut the car door and stood for a moment savoring the peace and the blessed coolness of the downland air. Bees hummed among the lime flowers above her, and a tabby cat rolled luxuriously in a fine clump of catmint in the sunny border.

Some distance away, Miriam discerned the figure of her new landlady. She was asleep in a deckchair, her head in the shade of a cherry tree, her feet propped up on a footstool in the sunshine.

Intense happiness flooded Miriam's being. The atmosphere of country tranquillity enveloped her

like some comforting cloak in bitter weather. Here
was home! Here was the peace she sought; the perfect antidote to the hectic atmosphere and pace of the
office!

Very quietly, she picked up her case and made her
way to the annex door.

🍂

Joan Benson woke with a start and looked at her
wrist watch. Almost four o'clock! Good heavens,
she must have slept for nearly two hours! Since her
mother's death she had found herself taking cat naps

like this, and friends told her that it was nature's way
of restoring her after the stress of tending the in-
valids of the family for so long.

She became conscious of faint noises from the annex. Of course, Miss Quinn would have arrived!
How shameful not to be awake to greet her!

She struggled from the deckchair, and hastened
towards the house to make amends. Miriam Quinn
received her apologies with a smile.

"I am going to make tea," said her new landlady.
"Do join me in the garden. You know that I want
you to look upon it as your own. Please feel free to
use it whenever you like. I have put up a little washing line for you, behind the syringa bushes. But I
will show you everything after tea."

She was as good as her word. Tea had obviously
been prepared with some care. There were home-
made scones, and tomato sandwiches, and some de-
licious shortbread. Miss Quinn could see that Joan
Benson was glad to have company, and was equally
anxious to be hospitable. She chattered happily as
she took her lodger round the garden, pointing out
new improvements which Ambrose had made, and
the herb patch which she herself had laid out.

"Take what you need," she urged. "There is
plenty here for both of us."

"You are very kind, Mrs. Benson."

"Oh, do please call me 'Joan,'" she cried. "We

surely know each other well enough for Christian names."

"Then you must call me 'Miriam,' " she responded.

"That's so much more friendly," agreed her landlady, leading the way back to the house. "You'll come in for a sherry later on, I hope."

Miriam chose to treat this as a question rather than a statement.

"I think I ought to get on with my unpacking, if you don't mind," she replied. "And I have one or two telephone calls to make."

"Of course, of course," agreed Joan warmly. "I think you'll find the extension telephone convenient in your sitting room. I very rarely use the one in my hall."

She bustled off to collect the tea tray and Miriam returned to the peace of her own small domain. She sat looking at the distant view from the window, and marshaling her thoughts.

She could be happy here, and Joan Benson was extremely kind and welcoming. Nevertheless, a small doubt disturbed her peace of mind.

Here they were, within one hour of her moving-in, on Christian name terms, and her head already throbbing with the pleasant but interminable chatter of her hostess. She was experienced enough to realize that a recently bereaved woman must be lonely and more than usually grateful for company. The thing was — was she willing to give the time and sympathy which Joan so obviously needed at the moment?

She recognized her own limitations. She liked her own company. She liked the tranquillity of her natural surroundings. She had more than enough people around her during office hours, and Holly Lodge she hoped would be her refuge from them. It would be sad if her contented solitude were shattered by the well-meaning overtures of her landlady.

She stood up abruptly, and began to sort out her books. She was going too fast! Of course, Joan would be extra forthcoming at their first meeting. She would be anxious to put her lodger at ease. She must respond as well as her more reserved nature would permit. Joan deserved much sympathy, and was tackling her difficulties with considerable bravery, Miriam told herself as she tried to come to terms with her new situation.

She lay in bed that night feeling the light breeze blowing across the miles of downland and cooling her cheeks. Somewhere a screech owl gave its eerie cry. A moth pattered up and down the window pane, and the fragrance from Joan's stocks scented the bedroom.

Miriam sighed happily. How quiet it was, after the noise of Caxley! What bliss to live here! She had not felt so free and relaxed since her far-off days in the Cambridgeshire vicarage.

It was all going to be perfect, she told herself sleepily. Quite perfect! Quite perfect — unless Joan became too —

She drifted into sleep.

※

She woke early and went to the window to savor the unbelievable freshness of the morning. Nothing stirred, except a pair of blackbirds busy among the rose bushes. A blue spiral of smoke rose in the distance. An early bonfire, the girl wondered? Or, more probably, the smoke from the chimney of a cottage hidden from view in a fold of the downs?

She bathed and dressed, relishing the privacy of her little house, and sat down to her toast and coffee soon after seven. There was no sound from next door, and she chided herself for feeling so relieved. Her need for solitude was even greater than usual first thing in the morning, and she sipped her coffee in contentment, looking around the kitchen and making a note of things yet to be done.

A rattling at the front door disturbed her train of thought. A letter lay on the mat, and as she picked it up she heard the postman pushing the mail through Joan's letterbox.

Her own sole missive was from Eileen, her sister-in-law, and consisted of two pages of good wishes for Miriam's future happiness in the new home, and news of the three children and Lovell, her husband and Miriam's only brother, two years her senior.

It was good of her to trouble to write, thought Miriam, but really, what an appalling hand she had, and why so many underlinings and exclamation marks? She poured out her second cup of coffee, and pondered on her sister-in-law's inability to buy envelopes which matched the writing paper, and to use a pen which wrote without dropping blots of ink. Such untidiness must irk Lovell as much as it did herself, for they were both neat and methodical, and had been so since childhood.

They had always been devoted to each other, and she remembered her grief when he had gone away to school. He had written regularly, in his neat small handwriting, so different from the untidy scrawl now before her.

From Cambridge he had followed his father into the Church, and was now vicar in a large parish, not far from Norwich, in the East Anglian countryside they both knew so well. Here he had met Eileen, soon after his arrival, and ever since then a certain bleakness had entered Miriam's life.

The old warm comradeship had gone, although no word was ever uttered. Miriam could understand her brother's love for the girl who so soon became his wife, but she could not help resenting her presence, try as she would.

Eileen was small and pretty, with an appealing air of fragility. Her fluffy fair hair was bound with ribbon. Her tiny shoes were bedecked with bows. She liked light historical novels, chocolate mints, deckleedged writing paper, and pale blue furnishings. She chattered incessantly and laughed a great deal. There was an air of teasing frivolity about her which would have earned her the title of "minx" in earlier days. She was a complete contrast to the sober and darkhaired Miriam and Lovell, and their earnest parents. It was hardly surprising that Lovell was captivated. He had never met anyone quite so adorable.

On the whole, the marriage had turned out well, despite the Quinns' private misgivings. Eileen had produced three attractive children, the youngest now almost two years old, and although they were allowed far too much license by their grandparents' standards, Miriam recognized that Eileen was a natural mother, quick to notice ailments and danger, although slapdash in her methods of upbringing. Her innate playfulness made her a good companion to the young things, and if discipline was needed — and often it was, for they were high-spirited children — then Lovell reproved them with due solemnity.

Yes, things could have been much worse, Miriam told herself, stacking the breakfast things neatly.

Lovell seemed happy enough, although one could not help wishing that he had found someone with a depth of character and outlook to match his own. But would she have liked such a woman any more than she liked Eileen?

She washed up thoughtfully, and was honest enough to admit that any woman whom Lovell married would have caused the same secret unhappiness. She had been supplanted, and it rankled. It was the outcome of unusual devotion between brother and sister, and she had now learned to live with this unpalatable fact.

She took a last look at herself in the long looking glass in her bedroom. Her thick dark hair was knotted on her neck. Her navy blue linen frock suited her slim build perfectly, and the plain but expensive shoes made an exact match. She looked what she was — an attractive, efficient business woman in her thirties.

"I wonder why she never married?" she had heard people say.

She wondered herself sometimes. There had been young men in her life, friends of Lovell's, for instance, when he was at Cambridge. Young and friendly, some of them ardent, they had been glad to visit the austere vicarage in the fens and to enjoy the homely hospitality offered there, and the company of Lovell's quiet young sister.

But, cool and farseeing, Miriam found none of them as attractive as the prospect of a life free of domestic responsibilities, free of children, and free of a lifelong partnership, which she doubted if she could sustain. With her upbringing, marriage would be for life, and sometimes, watching her hard-working mother, she wondered if she would ever be as selfless.

Single life had its compensations. If she had to stay late at the office, or decided to go straight from there to see a play in London, or to visit friends, then there was no one to inform or to consider. Her decisions needed no discussion with another. Everything was under control.

No one stirred next door as she drove her car towards the gate. The road was empty. The horizon as clear as her own mind. The day was mapped out. She knew exactly what would be happening at any given time. It was good to know where one was going.

Miriam Quinn was very sure of herself.

🌿

Within the next few weeks, news of the efficient paragon who lived in Mrs. Benson's annex had flashed round the village bush telegraph. Henry Mawne was largely to blame.

Gerald Partridge, the vicar, was in sore need of

someone to look after the books of the Church Fabric Fund. Henry Mawne, honorary secretary and treasurer to a score or more village concerns, stated flatly that he could not take on any more.

"But what about that nice Miriam Quinn?" he asked of his friend. "We met her the other night at Joan Benson's."

"But she must be very busy with her job," protested the vicar.

"She's home by about six. Why not ask her if she would like the job? She might be glad to meet people."

The same kindly thought had occurred to other people in Fairacre, particularly those on committees needing secretaries, treasurers, and that vague amorphous quality called "new blood." Here was a clever woman, obligingly free of family ties, in good health and possibly lonely, who could prove a godsend to the various organizations in need of help.

Henry Mawne was the first to approach Miriam on behalf of the short-staffed Church Fabric committee. She welcomed him to her shining house, gave him sherry, sparkled at his jokes, and declined the invitation in the most charming manner. Henry retired, hardly realizing that he had been defeated.

The Brownies needed a Brown Owl, the Cubs an Akela. The Women's Institute needed a bookkeeper as the last one still worked in shillings and pence, and in any case had lost the account book. The Over-Sixties' Club could do with a speaker on any subject, at any time suitable to Miss Quinn.

The Naturalists' Association, the Youth Club, the Play Group, the Welfare Clinic, St. Patrick's Choir, and the Sunday School were anxious to have Miss Quinn's presence and support, and Miriam soon realized, with amusement and resignation, that much more hummed beneath Fairacre's serene face than she had imagined.

Her tact, her charm, and her intelligence, backed by her formidable resolve to keep her life exactly as she wanted it, enabled her to stay clear of any of these entanglements.

Baffled, and slightly hurt, the villagers retired worsted.

Mrs. Pringle summed up the general feeling about the newcomer.

"No flies on Miss Quinn! She knows her own value, that one, but she ain't for sale!"

Chapter 3

NO HOLLY FOR MISS QUINN

*A*S THE WEEKS PASSED, Miriam's pleasure grew. Holly Lodge was all that she had hoped for — peaceful, convenient, and set among the great windswept countryside for which she had craved.

She took to strolling for an hour each evening before her supper. The air blew away the little tensions and annoyances of the office, and she always returned refreshed.

Sometimes she explored the village of Fairacre, stopping to talk politely to all who accosted her, but as Mr. Lamb at the Post Office said: "She don't make the running. It's you who has to start the conversation, though she's as nice as pie once you get going."

Henry Mawne and his wife she knew through her employer, and had been invited to their Queen Anne house at the end of the village on several occasions. The Hales at Tyler's Row, the Partridges at the vicarage, Mr. Willet, and Mrs. Pringle all were known to her, and she was on nodding terms with the majority of Fairacre's inhabitants.

But, on the whole, she preferred to ramble in the immediate vicinity of Holly Lodge. There she was unlikely to meet well-meaning folk who engaged her in conversation. She reveled in these solitary walks, noting the nuts and berries in the hedges, the flight of the downland birds, and the small fragrant flowers which flourished on the chalky soil.

She skirted the field of barley behind the house when she set off for the downs. Since her coming, the crop had turned from green to gold, fine and up-standing, with heavy ears. She watched it being har-vested in August, and listened to the regular thump-ing of the baler as she ate her simple evening meal in the sitting room or carried her tray to some quiet corner of the garden.

Joan Benson had quickly realized that the girl pre-ferred to be alone, and she sympathized with her feelings. After all, she told herself, Miriam arrived home tired, having dealt with people and their prob-lems all day.

She had met Sir Barnabas Hatch at the Mawnes' and had summed him up astutely as the sort of man who, endowed with twice the average amount of energy and intelligence, expects other people to be equally dynamic. Miriam could well hold her own, and her cool disposition would enable her to cope with any outbursts from her employer. Neverthe-less, he must be a demanding person with whom to deal, and it was no wonder that the girl needed the peace of her little home at the end of the day.

But although she respected Miriam's desire for privacy, she could not help feeling a little disappointed. She had hoped for company, and although the mere presence of someone next door was a great comfort, she sorely missed the conversation and company of her husband and mother. She found herself switching on the radio simply to hear another voice during the day, or making some excuse to walk to the village to enjoy a few words with anyone she met.

The days grew shorter. Joan tidied her garden, strung up her onions, planted bulbs, and had a massive autumn bonfire which wreathed blue smoke around Holly Lodge for two whole days. She was stirring the last of its embers one Saturday afternoon when Miriam waved to her from the other end of the garden.

"I'm off blackberrying," she called. "Shall I pick some for you?"

Joan dropped the hoe she had been using as an outsize poker, and hurried across.

"I'll join you, if I may," she said. "I've been meaning to go all the week. Wait half a minute while I fetch a basket."

Miriam rather welcomed company on this golden afternoon. She had finished the usual weekend chores of washing and shopping. The tradesmen had been paid their weekly dues, the house was clean. The mending awaited her, but otherwise her affairs were in as apple-pie order here as they were at the office. It would be good to hear Joan's news. She felt slightly guilty about seeing so little of her lately. This afternoon she would make amends.

The two women strode across the stubble of the field to a tall hedge. The sharp straw caught their legs, but it was wonderfully exhilarating to feel the crunch of it beneath their feet. At the farther edge of the field Miriam caught sight of something moving.

"Look!" she said, grasping Joan's arm. "A covey of partridges! There must be at least ten young ones running along there. I haven't seen that for a long time."

Joan was struck for the first time with the excitement in her companion's face.

"You really are a country girl!" she exclaimed. "Somehow I hadn't realized it."

Miriam smiled at her.

"It's why I love Holly Lodge so much," she told her.

The blackberries were thick and the two women picked steadily. Jet black, ruby red, and pale green, the berries cascaded down the hedge. United in their task, relaxed by the sunshine and sweet air, they talked of this and that, Miriam more forthcoming than ever before, and Joan relishing the chance to chatter again.

An onlooker might have learnt a great deal about the two women's natures, simply by watching their methods of picking. Miriam chose her bush with a shrewd eye to size and ripeness, and then picked swiftly and systematically, from the fat terminal berry, along the sides of the branch until all were gathered. Her movements were rapid but controlled, and not one berry was dropped.

Joan ambled happily between bushes, picking only the large ones. She lacked the concentration of the younger woman, but obviously enjoyed her haphazard forays and was quite content to have only half a basket of fruit, compared with Miriam's brimming one, when the time came to return home.

"I'm going to make tea," said Miriam. "Come and join me."

Joan was delighted to accept, and after depositing her basket in her own kitchen and washing her battle-scarred hands, she returned to the annex bearing some bronze chrysanthemums.

"I love them," said Joan, watching her neighbor arrange them, "but I always feel rather sad. They mean the summer's over. Still, they are very beautiful, and have such a marvelous scent. Rather like very expensive furniture polish, I always think."

Miriam let her chatter happily, wondering how to broach a subject which had been in her mind for some time.

"Would you mind if I redecorated these rooms, Joan?"

"Not at all," she said, looking a little surprised. "But they were done, you know, very recently."

"That's why I haven't liked to mention it. But, to tell you the truth, I'm not a lover of cream walls, and with this old mahogany I thought a very pale green would look well."

Joan nodded approvingly.

"It would indeed. Would you get somebody in

to do it? I'm sure Mr. Willet could recommend someone reliable. Shall I ask him?"

"No, there's no need. I shall enjoy tackling it myself. I'm quite experienced."

"What a lot of talents you have! When would you want to start? Can I help at all?"

Miriam began to feel the familiar qualms of apprehension returning.

"I may take a few days off," she said guardedly. "I have some time owing to me, and Barnabas has to make a trip overseas soon. I may be able to arrange something then. If not, I could probably do some of it at Christmas time."

This chance remark sent Joan along a new path.

"I'm writing to my two children this week to see if they can join me here for Christmas. I thought if they had plenty of notice, I should have more chance of their company. It would be lovely to have the house full and you could meet them all. Barbara's babies are such fun."

Miriam's heart sank.

"You're very kind," she murmured. "More tea?"

"I simply adore Christmas," continued Joan, stirring her second cup. "And Fairacre is the perfect place to spend it. Lots of little parties, and carol singers coming to the door and having a drink and mince pies when they've finished; and always such lovely services at St. Patrick's with the church decked beautifully with holly and ivy and Christmas roses. Christmas really is *Christmas* at Fairacre!"

Miriam's polite smile masked her inner misgivings. Christmas at the vicarage had always meant a particularly busy day for her father, and a considerable number of elderly relatives who had been invited by her kindly mother because as she said: "They had nowhere else to go, poor things, and one can't think of them alone at Christmas."

Miriam had long ago given up feeling guilty about her dislike of Christmas festivities, and latterly had taken pains to keep her own Christmases as quiet as possible. This year she was determined to spend it alone in her new abode, with no turkey, no pudding, no mince pies and — definitely — no holly.

She might have a glass of the excellent port that Barnabas usually gave her, with her customary light lunch, and she intended to read some Trollope, earmarked for the winter months. But too much food, too much noise and, above all, too much convivial company she would avoid.

But would she be able to?

She looked at dear kind Joan, rosy with fresh air and relaxed with warmth and company. How she blossomed, thought Miriam, with other people about!

No wonder she loved Christmas. Visiting, and being visited, was the breath of life to the good soul, and the joy of that festival would far outweigh any extra work which it entailed.

"I must be off," said Joan, struggling to her feet.

"There's bramble jelly to be made next door, and I must leave you to tackle your own."

Miriam closed the door behind her, and returned to the sitting room deep in thought.

It looked as though evading action might well be needed as Christmas approached.

She looked out upon the golden evening. The trees were beginning to turn tawny with the first cool winds of autumn.

Ah well, she told herself, time enough yet to postpone such troubles!

But the autumn slipped by at incredible speed. It was dark now when Miriam left the office. She was glad to nose her car into the garage and hurry into the annex to light the fire, which she prudently set in readiness in the morning.

The force of the equinoctial gales surprised her. Now she began to realize how open to the elements was this high downland country, and to appreciate the sagacity of the past owner of Holly Lodge who had had the foresight to plant the thick hedge that gave the house not only its name, but considerable protection from the blasts of winter.

Her own little home gave her increasing satisfaction. She had painted the kitchen white. It took three weekends of hard work to do the job, but Miriam was a perfectionist, and she rubbed down the old paint until not one scrap remained before she began to apply the undercoat with a steady hand. She enjoyed the work, she exulted in the finished result, and, above all, she relished the perfect quiet as she got on with the job.

She was even more determined now to tackle the sitting room at Christmas. Barney, as she thought of him, was making a business trip to Boston and New York, leaving on December sixteenth and not returning until after New Year's Day. Miriam had already made the flight bookings for him and Adele, his wife. They were meeting their only daughter, who was married to an American, and proposed to spend Christmas at her home and to see their grand-children. Miriam had been requested to find some toys suitable for children aged six and eight.

"The sort of thing they won't get over there, you know," said Barney vaguely. "Adele's got the main things, but I'd like to take something myself. I'll leave it to you. Not too weighty, of course, because of flying."

"I won't get an old English rocking horse," promised Miriam.

"Oh no! Nothing like that!" exclaimed Sir Barna-bas, looking alarmed. Humor, even as obvious as this, did not touch him. "And no more than five pounds apiece," he added. He was not a business man for nothing.

Miriam promised to do her best.

🍂

As Christmas approached, the whirl of village activities quickened. Posters went up on barn doors, on the trunks of trees, and on the bus shelter near the church, drawing attention to the usual Mammoth Jumble Sale, the Fur and Feather Whist Drive, and the Social and Dance, all to be held — on different dates, of course — under the roof of the Village Hall.

As well as these advertized delights, there were more private junketings, such as the Women's Institute Christmas party, Fairacre School's concert, and a wine and cheese party for the Over-Sixties' Club.

An innovation was Mrs. Partridge's Open Day at the vicarage, which was her own idea, and to which the village gave considerable attention.

"You can just pop in there," said Mrs. Willet, in the Post Office, "anytime between ten o'clock and seven at night. You pays ten pence to go in, and you pays for your cup of coffee, or your dinner midday, or tea, say, at four o'clock."

"And what, pray," said Mrs. Pringle, who was buying stamps, "do you get for dinner? And how much will it be?"

"I think it's just soup and bread and cheese," said Mrs. Willet timidly.

Mrs. Pringle snorted, and two stamps fluttered to the ground.

"I don't call that DINNER," boomed the lady, preparing to bend to retrieve the stamps.

"Here, let me," said Mr. Lamb, the postmaster, hurrying to rescue Mrs. Pringle's property. More than likely to have a heart attack, trying to bend over in those corsets, was his ungallant private comment, as he proffered the stamps with a smile.

"Ta," said Mrs. Pringle perfunctorily. She turned again upon little Mrs. Willet.

"And *how much* for this 'ere rubbishy snack?' "

"I'm not sure," faltered Mrs. Willet. "It's for charity, you see. Half to the Church Fabric Fund and half to some mission in London that the vicar takes an interest in. Poor people, you know."

"*Poor people?*" thundered Mrs. Pringle. "In London? Why, we've got plenty of poor in Fairacre as could do with a bit of help at Christmas, without giving it away to foreigners up London. Look at them Coggses! They could do with a bit of extra. That youngest looks half-starved to me."

"Well, whose fault's that?" asked Mr. Lamb, entering the fray. "We all know Arthur drinks his pay packet — always has done, and always will. If he was given more, he'd drink that too."

"Who said give Arthur the money?" demanded

Mrs. Pringle, her four chins wobbling with indigna-
tion. "Give it to that poor wife of his, I say, to get a
decent meal for the kids."

"They do get something from the Great Coal
Charity," said Mrs. Willet diffidently. Mrs. Pringle
brushed this aside.

"And in my mother's time she didn't rely on no
Great Coal Charity," she boomed on. "She paid her
way, poor though she was."

"She didn't have anything from the Great Coal
Charity," responded Mr. Lamb, "because there
wasn't one then."

"I'll have you know," said Mrs. Pringle with

devastating dignity, "that that there Charity was started in seventeen-fifty because the vicar told us himself at a talk he gave the W.I."

"Maybe," replied Mr. Lamb, "but it was started as a *Greatcoat Charity*, and six deserving old men and six deserving old women got a woolen greatcoat apiece to keep out the winter cold."

Mrs. Pringle looked disbelieving, her mouth downturned like a disgruntled turtle's.

"And what happened," said Mr. Lamb, warming to his theme, "was this. Someone left the crossing off the 't' in 'coat' when they were writing up the minutes about George the Fourth's time, and so it went on being called the Great Coal Charity, and instead of a coat you get coal."

"Well, I never," exclaimed Mrs. Willet. "I never heard that before!"

"Nor did I," said Mrs. Pringle, with heavy sarcasm. She picked up her stamps and made for the door.

"Which doesn't alter my feelings about bread and cheese dinners. What's dinner without a bit of meat on your plate?"

She banged the door behind her. Mrs. Willet sighed.

"That woman," said Mr. Lamb, "makes me come over prostrate with dismal when she shows that face of hers in here. Now, love, what was it you wanted?"

Chapter 4

TROUBLE AHEAD

MISS QUINN was wise enough to realize that
she could not opt out of Christmas activities completely. Nor did she wish to. She willingly
provided boxes of chocolates for raffle prizes at various Fairacre functions, accompanied Joan to a carol
service at St. Patrick's, and drank a glass of sherry
at the vicarage Open Day.

There was no doubt about it, this new venture was
extremely popular with Fairacre folk. Mrs. Partridge
and her helpers had decked the downstairs rooms
with scarlet and silver ribbons, and all the traditional
trappings of Christmas. Holly and ivy, mistletoe
and glittering baubles added their beauty, and an
enormous Christmas tree dominated the entrance
hall.

In each room was a table bearing goods suitable
for Christmas presents, and a brisk trade ensured
that the Church Fabric Fund and Mr. Partridge's pet
mission would profit. Miriam recognized the planning which must have gone into this enterprise, and

admired the efficiency with which it was run. It was an idea she intended to pass on to Lovell, when she saw him, for future use in his own parish.

These little jaunts she thoroughly enjoyed, and she was grateful for the genuine welcome she was given by her village neighbors. Joan's growing excitement, as the festival approached, was a source of mingled pleasure and apprehension, however.

"Isn't it wonderful?" Joan had said, on the morning of the Open Day. "Roger is coming for Christmas, after all, and then going with a party of other young people to Switzerland for the winter sports."

"Marvelous," agreed Miriam. Barbara, the daughter, her husband, and the three children had already accepted Joan's invitation and would be in the house for a week. Miriam had listened patiently to Joan's ecstatic arrangements for sleeping, feeding, and entertaining the family party for the last week or two. The plans were remarkably fluid, and Miriam had long since given up trying to keep track of who slept where, or when would be best to eat the turkey.

It was quite apparent that she must meet Joan's family at some time, and she had accepted an invitation to have a drink on Christmas Eve. So far, she had managed to evade the pressing invitations to every meal which her kindhearted landlady issued daily. That sitting room would be painted, come hell or high water, she told herself grimly.

She had arranged with Barney to take some time off during his absence in America. This would give her a few days before Christmas to get on with her decorating, having left the office in apple-pie order after his departure. Tins of paint and three new brushes waited on the top shelf in the kitchen, and she felt a little surge of happiness every time she saw them. She could see the sitting room in her mind's eye, a bower of green and white all ready for the New Year, and the new curtains and cushions she had promised herself.

Almost all her Christmas presents were wrapped and ready to post. Christmas cards began to arrive thick and fast. Usually, she had some plan of display — a whitewashed branch to hold them, or scarlet ribbons placed across the walls. But this year she read each with interest and then slipped it into a folder brought from the office, so that all were stacked away, leaving the sitting room ready for her ministrations.

She was glad when the time came to leave the office for her extended Christmas break. Four days after Barney's departure, with everything left tidy, she distributed her presents to the office staff, and thankfully set off for Fairacre and the decorating.

Lights were strung across the streets of Caxley, and entwined the lamp standards. Christmas trees jostled pyramids of oranges in the greengrocers'

shops. Turkeys hung in rows in the butchers', presenting their pink plump breasts for inspection.
Children flattened their noses against the windows
of the toy shops, while exhausted mothers struggled
with laden shopping baskets and wondered what
they had forgotten.

Queues formed at the Post Office: people buying
stamps for stacks of Christmas cards, weighing
parcels bedizened with Christmas stickers, or simply
enquiring, with some agitation, the last date for
posting to New Zealand and getting the answer they
had feared. Yet again, Aunt Flo in Wellington would
receive a New Year's card sent by air mail.

The surging crowds, the garish lights, the sheer
unappetizing commercialism of the festival disgusted
Miriam as she threaded her way slowly along the
busy streets. It was good to gain the country road
to Fairacre, climbing steadily towards the downs, to
smell the frosty air and to know that peace lay ahead,
behind the holly hedge.

She spent most of the evening by the fire, relishing her solitude and making plans for the attack on
the painting. She reviewed the situation and found
it highly satisfactory. Her posting was done. A box
containing Christmas presents, to be given by hand
to Joan and other local friends, was on a shelf in the
kitchen cupboard. The milkman was going to deliver
a small chicken in two days' time, ready for her

modest Christmas dinner. Christmas boxes for the
tradesmen waited on the hall window sill for distri-
bution as they called.

Nothing — but *nothing* — she told herself with
satisfaction, could keep her from her decorating
now!

Fired by the thought, she began to gather together
the ornaments about the room, stacking them in a
large cardboard box. It would save time in the morning, when she would roll up the carpet, take down
the curtains and push the large pieces of furniture
into the center of the room. Already she had found
two dust sheets to cover the mound, and had planned
the best method of building the assorted shapes of
sofa, chairs and table into a compact pile. Her
methodical mind reveled in such practical arrangements. The job was going to be as efficiently tackled
as any at the office, and would give her far more
satisfaction.

She prepared the room next morning, and by
midday was down to the exacting job of washing
down the old paint, and rubbing down any uneven
patches on the surface. Joan came in once or twice
to see if there was anything she could do to help.
Miriam greeted her with a smile, but was obviously
so content to work alone that Joan retired after
expressing admiration for Miriam's zeal.

"It's going to look marvelous," she cried. "Will
you have lunch with me? It will save you cooking."

"I've made a sandwich," replied Miriam, "and shall have it with some coffee to save time, if you don't mind."

Joan was secretly rather relieved. Her whole attention now was on the arrival of Barbara and family in two days' time. After the loneliness of the past months, it was pure joy for her to be preparing food and decking the house, in readiness for the company which would bring Holly Lodge to life again.

Christmas Day fell on a Thursday. Miriam had high hopes of finishing the painting by then, although she faced the fact that the windows — always a tricky and tedious job — might have to be left for later. As Barney would not be back from America until January third, she had planned to take another few days after Christmas if all were well at the office. There should be ample time to get the sitting room into perfect order.

By Monday evening the first coat of emulsion paint was on the walls. She stood back, brush in hand, to admire its delicate shade. Yes, it was perfect!

Tomorrow she would put on the second and final coat, she told herself happily, going to the sink to rinse the paint brush. She could hear Joan talking to someone on the telephone. No doubt Barbara was ringing about the traveling plans.

But a moment later, Joan called to her.

"Your brother, Miriam, from Norfolk."

"Right!" called the girl, drying her hands.

Lovell sounded agitated.

"I've trouble here," said the deep voice. "Eileen's just gone to hospital."

"An accident?"

"No, nothing like that. But most acute stomach pains. Awful sickness. Probably something to do with the gall bladder. She's had this sort of thing off and on for some time, but this morning she had this really terrible attack."

"Poor Eileen! Where is she? Far away?"

"No. In the local hospital. The thing is, can you possibly come and hold the fort for the next few days? I know it's asking a lot, but over Christmas I shall be extra busy in the parish, and I don't know which way to look for help with the children."

"I can come," said Miriam promptly. It was good to know that Lovell turned at once to her when he needed help. The old strong bond between them was reestablished in those few words uttered so many miles apart.

"You're a trump, Miriam," cried Lovell. The relief in his voice warmed her heart. "I can't tell you how glad I am. And so will the children be, and Eileen, when I tell them."

"I'll set off first thing," said Miriam, "and be with you tomorrow afternoon. Have you got provisions in, or shall I bring something?"

"Oh, I expect everything's here," said Lovell, but he sounded somewhat vague.

There was a sound of infant screaming in the background.

"Don't worry," called Miriam hastily: "I'll see to things when I arrive."

"Marvelous!" sighed her brother.

The screaming became louder. Miss Quinn replaced the receiver and went sadly back to the half-painted sitting room.

"Well," she said glumly. "That's that!"

Joan heard the news with distress. Anything to do with illness touched her sympathetic heart, and reawakened memories of her own two recent bereavements. On this occasion there were further causes for dismay.

"And at Christmas too! And with children in the home! Dear, oh dear, it couldn't be more unfortunate, especially with the extra services your brother will have to take. If only I could help!"

"I know you would if you could, but you will have enough to do at Holly Lodge. I will telephone as soon as I get there tomorrow."

There was nothing more to do to the painting until the first coat was thoroughly dry. It should certainly be just that by the time she returned, she thought grimly. Understandable irritation began to flood her as she packed away the brushes and tins. How like Eileen to manage to mess up so many people's affairs!

Immediately, she chided herself, but the resentment remained to rankle as she found her case and began to pack. And yet, in a distorted way, she almost felt grateful to Lovell's wife for giving her the chance to have his company for a few days of uninterrupted pleasure. It was years since they had been able talk without the presence of her flibbertigibbet sister-in-law.

It took her longer to pack than usual. Clearing the

sitting room had meant stacking things in unaccustomed places, and she was hard put to it to find a map showing the route. At last it turned up, packed among cookery books. Yes, skirt Oxford, make for Bicester, Buckingham, Bedford, Cambridge, Newmarket, and then on into Norfolk. It was going to be a longish trip. She must start at first light, and pray for a fine day. There was no knowing what she would find to do when she arrived, and she only hoped that the bitter winter weather, for which East Anglia was noted, would hold off and enable her to return in good time. Oh, that poor sitting room, she grieved!

She climbed into bed, turned out the light, and determined to put aside tomorrow's worries and get to sleep. The vision of a raddled old housemaid called, unbelievably, Euphrosyne, who had helped at her parents' vicarage, came into her mind.

"What can't be cured must be endured," was one of her favorite sayings.

Maybe Euphrosyne had the last word there, thought Miriam, settling to sleep.

There was frost on the grass when Miriam looked out first thing in the morning. It was gray and still, overcast, but bitterly cold. In the fold of the downs, scarves of mist floated. No breeze stirred the bare

branches, and the birds sat huddled in silence, awaiting any largesse thrown from the kitchen window.

It was a dispiriting sort of day, thought Miss
Quinn, brewing her coffee. She only hoped that the
mists of Fairacre were not an indication of fog in the
flat fields of Bedfordshire and the fen lands beyond.

She remembered the chill of Lovell's drafty
vicarage, and went to hunt for two extra thick
sweaters to throw into the back of the car with her
Wellington boots. Brought up in that bleak area of
England, she prudently went prepared for the worst
that the weather could do in December.

Joan called in soon after nine, bearing fruit,
biscuits, and a flask of coffee.

"I hope I'm in time. Have you made some sandwiches?"

"Well, no," admitted Miriam, after thanking her.
"I thought I would stop on the way and have a
proper lunch. I shall be ready for it, no doubt, and
heaven alone knows if there will be anything prepared at Lovell's. I'm taking eggs for us all, to be on
the safe side."

"Good. Do ring as soon as you arrive. I shall be
anxious."

"I will. And do use my bedroom while the family
is here, if it's any help. I have stripped the bed."

Joan's face lit up.

"That would be marvelous, if you're sure. Roger

could go there, or I could perhaps. How nice of you! I will work it out while I'm making the mince pies this morning.''

It was plain that this new turn would add agreeably to her multifarious plans, and Miriam was glad to see her so occupied.

By half-past nine she was on her way, having said farewell to Joan and left her Christmas presents. The hedges were hoary with rime, and in each dip of the downs the mist still swirled. Thin ice crackled beneath the car wheels, and the whole world looked cold and unwelcoming. She thought with longing

of the snug cottage she had left behind, and of the
work half done.

> But duty, duty must be done,
> The rule applies to everyone,
> And painful though that duty be
> . To shirk the task is fiddle-de-dee,

she sang aloud, cheering herself with the thumping
rhythm, as the car sped onward.

To her relief, a watery sun, pallid as the moon,
became visible through the clouds as she rattled
along the road which by-passed Oxford. On each
side lay water meadows, and the leaden sheen of the
winding river, its course marked by willows stark
in their winter nakedness.

As the sun's strength increased, so did Miss
Quinn's spirits rise. It was good to see something
different. Good to be visiting Lovell, even in such
worrying circumstances. Good, even, to feel unaccustomed sympathy for the tiresome Eileen who
had precipitated this journey. Looking after the
three children Miriam viewed with some trepidation.
They were healthy, high-spirited youngsters, and
would no doubt be missing their mother. Miriam
knew her limitations. She might be Barney's right
hand. She might be the dragon that frightened the
typing pool. Whether she would be as efficient as
aunt-cum-housekeeper remained to be seen.

Bicester and Buckingham were passed. Strange, alien Wolverton, an industrial surprise among the flat fields, lay behind her. After Newport Pagnell, she told herself, she would find a likely looking lane to enjoy Joan's coffee and fruit. Hunger began to assail her, but the sun now shone warmly, and the midlands, which Hilaire Belloc had found "sodden and unkind," lay ahead bathed in gentle sunlight.

She turned into a by-lane where the hedge maple gleamed like gold. A robin flew onto a nearby twig, watching her closely. Crumbs had been known to come from car windows.

Miriam crushed one of Joan's biscuits and scattered it for her companion, who darted down to enjoy this unexpected feast.

Watching his sharp beak at work, Miriam sipped her steaming coffee. In amicable silence, the two strangers enjoyed their meal together.

Chapter 5

A WELCOME FOR MISS QUINN

S HE BROKE HER JOURNEY at Cambridge, partly because the place was full of happy memories of her own and Lovell's youth and, more practically, because she knew exactly where to go shopping.

She was lucky to find a parking space outside Queen's. Here, at a May Week ball long ago, she had met Martin Farrar, a friend of Lovell's, and had enjoyed a few weeks' mild flirtation with the handsome boy. Where was he now, she wondered? Farming somewhere in a nearby county, she seemed to remember Lovell saying one day — and happily married.

It was bitingly cold, despite the sunshine. The slow-moving Cam was dappled with the last yellow leaves of autumn, and a vicious little wind stirred the dust along Silver Street.

She bought fruit, bacon, and sausages, enough to provide a supper and a breakfast and to give her time to check the provisions in Eileen's store cupboard.

She also bought a bottle of sherry for Lovell and flowers for the invalid; and, at the last minute, dived into a shabby toy shop for crayons and balloons. Thus armed she returned to the car, and having deposited her purchases, decided to treat herself to a splendid lunch at the Garden House hotel nearby.

She was on her way again, much fortified, within the hour.

As always, the miles seemed longer than ever after Newmarket, as the wide heathlands stretched away into the distance, and the well-known East Anglian wind scoured the countryside.

It was almost dark by the time she arrived at the vicarage.

No one answered the bell which she pressed hopefully at the front door, so she pushed it open, to be greeted by a pungent smell of burning.

The wide hall ran from front door to a glass one at the back. Through it Miriam could see the shabby overgrown garden backed by a lowering sky.

Light spilled from a side door into the hall, and she could hear children laughing. Obviously, all activity was centered in the kitchen.

"Anyone home?" she called, advancing, her heels clicking on the black and white marble tiles. Not even a rush mat, thought Miss Quinn, to mitigate the piercing cold to one's feet!

There were screams of excitement as two little girls tumbled through the door, and rushed upon her.

"Auntie Miriam! You've come! We thought you'd be here when we'd gone to bed!"

Two pairs of sticky hands caressed her new Welsh tweed suit lovingly. She bent to kiss the children. The extraordinary smell seemed to envelop them.

"We're making toffee," said Hazel importantly.

"Only it's a bit caught," added Jenny. "Come and see."

She followed them into the kitchen. Hazel, the nine-year-old, led her to the electric stove. Jenny, two years younger, indicated the saucepan, and Miriam's heart plummeted.

A tarlike substance coated one of the open ele-ment electric plates, and made rivulets down the once white front of the stove.

The residue gleamed malevolently from the bot-tom of a buckled saucepan. That was one utensil, thought Miriam, which would have to be replaced.

"Where is the toffee?" she inquired.

"It's here, you see, but we just ran out into the garden to tell Daddy the telephone was ringing, and it all went sort of fizzy and buzzled all over the stove."

"That's right," corroborated Jenny, licking a sticky finger. "It tastes funny, but it's set, hasn't it?"

"It certainly has," said Miriam with distaste. "Put it in the sink to soak."

"But it's *toffee*," wailed Jenny, sensing adult disapproval. "We can *eat* it! There's a pound of sugar in it."

"There's a pound of sugar," agreed Miriam, "but it's mostly over the stove. Cheer up, I'll make you some fudge instead. But where's Daddy?"

"He went to find Robin. He's in the garden somewhere. We'll show you."

She followed their prancing figures into the dusky garden. Both children were dark-haired, like their father, but she could not believe that she and Lovell had ever been quite so thin.

Did Eileen feed them properly, or were they allowed to leave food if they were too impatient to eat it? Time would tell.

In any case, they were not lacking in energy. They hopped and skipped ahead of her, leaping over brambles and tussocks of grass that must once have been a lawn in more spacious days.

"She's come! Daddy, she's come!" screamed the little girls, and out from behind a hedge, came Lovell holding his youngest in his arms.

"You dear girl!" he cried, depositing Robin at his feet. He put his arms round Miriam in a bear hug. They had never been demonstrative, and this welcoming embrace made all the irritations of the journey drop away. His face was cold, his hair rough and smelling of all outdoors. A wintry, bruised-grass, autumn-bonfire smell, as different from the

acrid scent of burning which had greeted her as sea-mist is from midland fog.

In that instant, she was transported back to their shared childhood when together they climbed trees, or rolled, screaming with delight, down a grassy slope in the vicarage garden. Sudden tears pricked her eyes, and Lovell, holding her now at arm's length, said:

"You look cold. Come inside."

The two little girls bounced ahead, but Robin held up his arms to be carried. Miriam watched Lovell hoist him aloft again, and thought how like his mother the young boy looked. He had the same fair hair and blue eyes, the wide brow and pointed chin which gave Eileen her childlike air.

She held out a hand to him, but he turned away from her, burying his face in his father's neck.

"That's no way to welcome an aunt," chided Lovell. "Why, she's going to be the angel in the house, if only you knew it!"

"Wait and see!" laughed Miriam, following her brother indoors.

It seemed to Miriam, as she surveyed the sitting room where most of the family activities went on, that a strong charwoman, rather than an angel, was needed in the place.

Toys littered the table, the chairs, and the carpet. Copper, the aging cocker spaniel, was curled up on the rumpled cover of the couch in front of the fire. A log had rolled off, and lay smoldering in the hearth, filling the room with pungent smoke. A glass vase containing six dead chrysanthemums and an inch of dark green slime decorated the mantelpiece, with a half-eaten banana beside it.

Lovell, dropping Robin beside the spaniel, caught sight of his sister's face, and laughed.

"Ghastly, isn't it? We had a sort of scratch lunch, and that banana is Robin's contribution."

"Well," said Miriam, trying to sound briskly cheerful, "that can soon be put right. What's happened to Annie?"

Annie was a young girl from the village who came for a couple of hours or so in the late afternoon each day to help Eileen with the children's tea and bath time.

"She's off over Christmas," explained Lovell. "The family has gone to Ely to stay with the grandmother, but she will be back on Monday, I hope."

Miriam hoped so too. She bent to remove a grubby handkerchief from Robin's grasp. He was busy wiping Copper's nose, and the dog resented it. The child set up an ear-splitting wail, and the two little girls rushed to comfort him.

Miriam hastily returned the handkerchief, and the wailing ceased as though a siren had been switched off.

"Perhaps I'd better take up my case," she said to Lovell, "and then I will cook a meal for us all."

"Goody-goody!" shouted Hazel.

"Gum-drops!" yelled Jenny. "That's what we say: 'Goody-goody-gum-drops!' Do you say that? Do you say: 'Goody-goody-gum-drops!' when you're pleased? We do, don't we, Hazel? We *always* say: 'Goody-goody —' "

"Not now you don't," said Lovell firmly. "Let Aunt Miriam have a few minutes' peace. Shall I take you up?"

"No, no," replied Miriam hastily, "I expect I'm in the usual room, aren't I?"

"I'll come with you," said Jenny.

"No, let me!" said Hazel.

"*Only one!*" bellowed Lovell, above the din. "You show Aunt Miriam to her room, Hazel, and then come down again. We'll set the table in the kitchen."

Miriam deposited her basket of groceries on the kitchen dresser, averting her eyes from the appalling state of the stove. Hazel was swinging on the newel post at the foot of the stairs, her dark hair flying behind her.

"Daddy's going to see Mummy this evening," she announced, prancing up the stairs in front of Miriam. "Can I go too?"

With a shock, Miriam realized that she had forgotten to ask after the mistress of the house in the turmoil of her arrival.

"We must ask Daddy," said she diplomatically. "The hospital staff may not want too many visitors all at once."

"But why not? I bet my mummy would like to see me, and I could tell her about the toffee we made, and having bread and peanut butter for lunch today."

By now they had traversed the long passage over the hall and Hazel flung open the door of the spare room. The light switch failed to work.

Miriam set down her heavy case and groped her

way to a bedside table where she remembered that a reading lamp stood. Mercifully, it worked. Obviously, the main light needed a new bulb. She must see about that later on.

The room was cold and musty, and it was apparent that neither of the twin beds was made up. Lumpy rectangles composed of folded blankets showed through the candlewick bedspreads. She must face that job as soon as the children were in bed, and put in a hot bottle if she were to escape pneumonia in this chilly Norfolk climate. She had a strong suspicion that this room had not been used since her last visit in the early summer.

"Shall I help you to unpack?" enquired Hazel, eyeing the case hopefully.

"No. I'll do it later. You run downstairs and help Daddy. I'm just coming."

She hung up her coat on a peg on the back of the door. There was no coat hanger to be seen in the clothes' cupboard. What a house, thought Miriam! A vision of her own neat domain floated before her, and she had to wrench her mind to other matters to overcome the sudden flood of depression which engulfed her.

The bathroom was next door, chillier even than her own room. The bath was grimy. The wash basin was worse, and had what looked like a used medical plaster, recently stripped from someone's damaged finger, stuck to a cracked piece of soap. Miriam gingerly picked up this revolting amalgam and dropped it into an ancient enamel slop pail which seemed to do service as a wastepaper basket. Luckily, the bath rack provided her with a large tablet of Lifebuoy soap, and she was grateful for its disinfectant properties.

She unpacked a clean overall which she had prudently brought with her, and descended the stairs.

Lovell was slicing bread at the dresser, and Robin was sitting on the floor at his feet eating the crumbs that fell.

"Is it tea or supper?" asked Jenny. Miriam looked at Lovell.

"As they had so light a lunch," she said, "what about eggs and bacon? And sausages if you like. Do they have a meal like that before bedtime?"

"Oh, yes! Yes! We *always* have something like that, don't we?"

Their faces were rapturous. It was quite plain that they were hungry.

Lovell found her the frying pan, which was surprisingly clean, and she set about unpacking and cooking the provisions she had brought with her. Lovell, unasked, opened an enormous tin of baked beans and within twenty minutes Miriam's first meal was on the table.

There had been little culinary art in providing it and still less finesse in presenting it, straight from the pan to the waiting plates, but the children's evident relish as they demolished the meal gave her infinite satisfaction.

Now she found time to make amends and enquire after the patient.

"I'll know more when I've seen her this evening," said Lovell. "I'll help you to put this mob to bed and drive over to the hospital. You won't mind being left?"

"Of course not. I'll go tomorrow to see her."

"At the moment she is under observation, I gather. She's on a pretty strict diet, and having tests. If that doesn't have any result, then they'll think of surgery."

"What's surgery?" asked Hazel.

"It's cutting people up," explained Jenny kindly. "Like making chops at the butcher's."

At this point, Robin turned his mug upside down on the tablecloth and watched the milk creep towards the edge.

"He always does that when he's finished," said Jenny indulgently. "Isn't he a funny boy?"

Miriam rose to fetch a dishcloth, and began to mop up the mess. Only Lovell's presence restrained her from giving a sharp reprimand to the drowsy Robin, who now leant back sucking his thumb.

The little girls watched her efforts with interest.

"We bathed Copper with that cloth this afternoon. He was smelly, so we *squeezed* it out in soapy water, and gave him a *lovely* wash."

Miriam stopped her labors abruptly, and transferred the cloth to a battered tidy-bin beneath the sink. At this rate, she thought, a packet of J cloths must take priority on tomorrow's shopping list.

"We'll wash up," said Lovell, rising to his feet, "and I think Robin's ready for bed if you could cope with him."

At this, the comatose boy became instantly alert and shook his head violently.

"No! Dadda do! Dadda do!" he yelled, scarlet in the face.

"I think you'd better tonight," said Miriam swiftly. "He'll be more obliging when he knows me. We'll clear up here."

The two males vanished, and Miriam and the girls set about making order out of chaos. There seemed to be a dearth of tea cloths and a decidedly vague idea of where they were kept.

"They just hang about," said Hazel. "On the back of that chair usually."

"I mean the *clean* ones," said Miriam, her voice sharp with exasperation.

"I think they're in this drawer," said Jenny, struggling with an overfull dresser drawer stuffed with jam pot covers, pieces of string, two soup ladles, and what looked like half a colander. A few pieces of tattered cloth were intermingled with debris and, after close inspection, proved to be extremely ancient tea cloths.

"Aren't you getting excited about Christmas?" inquired Jenny, patting a spoon with one of the tattered rags, as her contribution to wiping the cutlery. "I am. I've asked Father Christmas for a painting set. Lots of different pots and brushes."

"I hope you'll get them," said Miriam civilly.

"Oh, she'll get them," announced Hazel, in a meaning way, "but whether *Father Christmas* will bring them, I don't know."

Jenny's face became suffused with angry color.

"Of course he'll bring them! My letter to him

went *straight* up the chimney! Yours fell back and got burnt up, and serves you right."

"Now, now," said Miriam warningly. Really, she thought, I sound just like my mother! How stupid "Now, now!" sounded! Almost as idiotic as "Now then," a phrase which could bring on partial madness if considered for too long.

It was quite apparent that Hazel was wise to the myth of Santa Claus, while her sister was still touchingly a believer in the Christmas fairy. She must try and get a quiet word with the older child before too much damage was done.

Lovell reappeared as they were finishing. He looked exhausted and Miriam's heart was smitten.

"Go and sit by the fire, and I'll bring you some coffee," she said. "You don't need to set off immediately, do you?"

"Visiting hours are seven until eight-thirty," he said. "Goodness, it looks clean in here! I didn't give Robin a bath, just washed his face and hands. He's asleep already."

Scandalized, the little girls spoke together.

"But Robin *always* has a bath!"

"Annie *always* does him all over! He needs a bath."

"Mummy says we *must* have a bath before bed. Robin won't like it when he wakes up and finds he's all dirty still."

"He won't wake up," said their father shortly.

"We'll give him an extra long one tomorrow," promised Miriam, setting the kettle to boil, "as it's Christmas Eve!"

When Lovell had drunk his coffee and departed, carrying Miriam's bouquet and some magazines for Eileen, she took the girls up to the bathroom and bribed them into the steaming bath with one of her precious bath cubes.

"I'll come back in ten minutes to see if you are really clean," she told them, and left them to their own devices while she unpacked her case.

Later, scrubbed and sweet-smelling in their flowered night gowns, they held up their arms for a goodnight kiss, and Miriam admitted to herself that just now and again — for very brief periods — children could be very winning.

She descended the long staircase feeling a hundred years old. Fairacre and Holly Lodge seemed light-years away. This reminded her that she had promised to ring Joan.

But not before she had revived herself with coffee, she told herself, making for the kitchen. Peremptory barking greeted her. Copper stood pointedly by his empty plate.

"Amazingly enough," Miriam told him, "I know where your supper is!"

She tipped out the remains of a tin of dog food she had noticed in the larder, and Copper wolfed it down with relish.

He accompanied her to the fireside when she sank into her armchair with the cup of coffee and attempted to climb on her lap.

"Some other time, Copper, old boy," said Miriam faintly, fending him off. "It's as much as I can do to support myself."

She lay back and listened to the little domestic sounds of the old house. The fire whispered, a log shifted at its heart, the dog snored gently after his meal. Outside, the wind stirred the trees, and somewhere a distant door banged as the breeze caught it.

Gradually, the peace that surrounded her took effect. It had been a long day, and tomorrow would be an even harder one. But meanwhile, the children slept as soundly as the dog on the rug at her feet, and the night enfolded the quiet house.

When Lovell returned, he found his sister fast asleep in the arm chair.

Chapter 6

A CHRISTMAS MEMORY

Miss Quinn woke with a start, and sat bolt upright in bed.

Close at hand a church clock was striking midnight, and its pulsing rhythm filled the room.

Bewilderment and panic ebbed away, as she lay down again. Of course, she was safe in her brother Lovell's vicarage! This spare room, she remembered now, was close to the church tower.

It must be frosty tonight to be able to hear so clearly. Morning light would show rimy grass, no doubt, and ice-covered puddles, the little birds huddled patiently on sparkling twigs awaiting any bounty flung from the kitchen door.

The last stroke died away, and the old house sank back into silence. Sleep enveloped Lovell and the three children whom she had come to look after over Christmas, whilst their mother was in the hospital.

Poor Eileen, she thought! Was she asleep too, or lying awake, as she was herself? She envisaged the shadowy ward, a night nurse sitting in the one small pool of light, alert for any sound from a restless patient. How much luckier she was, to be here alone and free from pain!

With a sudden shock, she realized that it was now Christmas Eve. There would be wild excitement from her two nieces in the next few hours. Robin would be too young to understand, though no doubt he would be infected by the general fever of anticipation. Did the children hang up stockings here, she wondered, or pillow cases, as she and Lovell had done, in just such a drafty vicarage years ago?

One Christmas in particular she recalled vividly in that old Cambridgeshire house. She must have been about the same age as young Jenny asleep next door. Her milk teeth were beginning to wobble, and one in the front, she remembered, had been tipped back and forth so often by her questing tongue that her mother had begged her to "pull it out and have done with it." But fear had held her back, and even Lovell's pleas to "give it a good jerk" were in vain.

Lovell, two years older, was young Miriam's hero. He could climb to the top of their yew tree, while she stuck, trembling, half-way. He could make a whistle with his penknife and a hollow reed. He had bloodied Billy Boston's nose when he swore about their father, and he learnt geometry at the new day school in Cambridge.

Whatever Lovell did, Miriam tried to do. What-

ever Lovell told her, she believed implicitly. Whatever Lovell said was right, was so, and whatever
Lovell found wrong was, of course, quite wrong.

This particular Christmas Miriam was much exer-
cised in her mind. Ruby, her six-year-old friend at
school, had stated categorically that there was no
Father Christmas. Miriam was horrified at such an
infamous statement.

"Of course there is! You get presents don't you?"

Ruby, skipping busily at the time, was offhand.

"Your mum or dad puts 'em there," she puffed,
twirling the rope.

"I don't believe it," said Miriam stoutly, but a
cold hand seemed to clutch at her stomach. Could it
be true? Could her father and mother have told her
lies? Could Lovell?

Never, she told herself! Lovell always told her the
truth. If there were no Father Christmas Lovell
would have said so. It was Ruby who told lies.

"You don't know what you're talking about," she
told the skipper robustly. "I just *know* there's a
Father Christmas, so there!"

"Better stay awake and find out," shouted Ruby to
Miriam who was walking away.

And maybe I will, thought Miriam stubbornly,
just to prove she's wrong.

In the few days left before Christmas she was
often on the point of asking her mother about this

problem. But, as always, the vicarage was fast filling up with elderly relatives who were coming to spend Christmas with the family, and Mrs. Quinn was fully occupied.

"Poor things," said that warm-hearted lady to her husband. "They've nowhere to go, and it's quite unthinkable that they should be alone at a time like this." The Reverend Horace Quinn, that staunch Christian, readily agreed.

Both parents replied kindly to Miriam's tentative enquiries about the authenticity of Father Christmas, but were vague and preoccupied. On the whole, though, she felt slightly reassured.

Among the Christmas guests was a recently widowed young aunt with her four-year-old son Sidney. The child was delicate, and made even more so by his mother's mollycoddling.

"Naturally she fusses over him," Miriam heard her mother say to one of the elderly second cousins. "He's all she has now, and he is a dear little boy."

Lovell and Miriam did not think so. They thought him spoilt, a cry-baby and a tale-teller. The fact that the poor child lisped only made him more ridiculous in their eyes. With childish heartlessness they teased the little boy, without mercy, whenever they had him alone.

It so happened that this particular Christmas Eve brought snow to bleak East Anglia, and the three chil-

dren were wrapped up warmly and sent to play, with injunctions to make a snowman. Lovell and Miriam, strong and boisterous, threw themselves into the task joyfully, but Sidney, half-afraid of the bigger children and disliking the cold, did little.

"Come on, Thid," shouted Lovell, "lend a hand!"

"Thid, Thid, Thilly-Thid-Thid!" mocked Miriam, following Lovell's lead as usual.

The child shook his head unhappily, near to tears. Irritated by his apathy, the two young savages began to chase him round and round the half-built snow-man. Within two minutes the little boy was sobbing, and struggling to escape from his tormentors. They pursued him ruthlessly, until at last he fell wailing into the snowman and the bigger children, incensed at the damage, rolled the child back and forth in the snow.

"Now look what you've done!"

"All our work spoilt! We'll pay you out for this!"

They began stuffing snow down the neck of the child's jersey, giggling now, but still enjoying the feeling of power over this weakling.

Sidney's cries attracted his mother. The three children were driven into the kitchen and the young Quinns were accused by Sidney's hysterical mother of gross cruelty. Mrs. Quinn banished her two to their bedrooms for an hour, after apologies all round, and Miriam spent the time wobbling the front tooth and thinking about the existence, or otherwise, of Father Christmas.

Called down to tea after their penance, Miriam spoke urgently to Lovell as they went into the dining room.

"Ruby Adair at school said there wasn't a Father Christmas. Is it true?"

An extraordinary look came over Lovell's face. It was as though Miriam had hit him. He stuttered when he replied, a thing he only did when very upset.

"You don't want to believe everything Ruby says," he managed to say. "I've never told you that, have I?"

The tension, which had screwed Miriam's inside

into a painful knot, lessened at once, and the feeling
of relief carried her through the hours until bedtime.
She even managed to speak kindly to the loathsome
Sidney who insisted on sitting close to his mother.

Bedtime came. The three children prepared the
traditional snack for Father Christmas, a mince pie
from each one, and a glass of orange squash, which
Sidney chose as the best drink available.

Miriam watched Lovell closely as they placed the
food in the hearth. His face was solemn, and he was
being uncommonly gentle with young Sidney. He
would not take such trouble, thought Miriam with
relief, if he did not truly expect Father Christmas to
arrive.

The children went to bed. Over each bed rail hung
an empty pillowcase. Miriam looked at hers as she
lay awake. If, as silly Ruby said, one's parents filled
it then she would be bound to hear them.

Despite her intention to stay alert, she was asleep
in ten minutes. The sound of the door opening woke
her, hours later.

"All right?" she heard her mother whisper.

Her father answered:

"Fast asleep!"

Cold with horror, she lay motionless.

She saw the empty pillowcase twitched from the
bed rail, and felt the bump of a full one as it was
lodged at the foot of the bed. So *that* was how it was
done!

The door closed noiselessly. She lay there, numbed with shock. A painful lump swelled in her throat, and hot tears began to trickle. Ruby was right.

To think that all this time her parents had lied! And Lovell too! It was cruel. All these years she had loved Father Christmas, and now it was spoilt.

She crept from her bed, and squatting on the floor, she felt the various shapes in the pillowcase. There was the doll she had asked for, and this box must be the tea set or a jigsaw puzzle. She could smell the fragrance of the tangerine tucked in a corner, and could hear the rattle of the nuts in the other.

Tears continued to course down her cheeks. She would not unpack things until morning light. And would she enjoy them then, she wondered, knowing that Lovell had betrayed her? Would things ever be the same again?

Her feet were cold as stones, and she clambered back into bed. As she did so, her restless tongue finally broke the loose tooth from its precarious moorings. Still weeping, she felt the edge of the new tooth thrusting through. She pulled the clothes about her, and fell into an uneasy sleep.

Leaden-eyed and leaden-hearted next morning, she did her best to share in the general excitement.

At the breakfast table she thanked all her relatives for their gifts. She could hardly bear to look at Lovell, so happy and unconcerned.

Sidney was flushed with joy and excitement.

"All gone!" he said, showing her Father Christmas's empty plate. "Did you thee him?"

He pressed against Miriam anxiously.

"Did you thee him?" he persisted.

Conscious of the eyes of all upon her, her heart raging with bitterness, Miriam took a deep breath. She turned her blazing gaze upon the traitor Lovell.

"No, I *didn't!*" she burst forth. "I *didn't* see Father Christmas, Sidney. But I'll tell you what I *did* see!"

The child looked up at her, smiling and trusting.

Lovell's gaze was steady. Across the breakfast table, brother and sister were locked in a look.

Very slowly Lovell shook his head. Briefly, and with a wealth of meaning, he glanced at Sidney, and then looked back at Miriam. It was a conspiratorial look, and it filled Miriam's quivering body with warmth and comfort. Now, in a flash, she understood. Suddenly, she was grown up. Hadn't she felt the first of her adult teeth this very morning?

A little child, as she had been until now, had the right to believe in this magic. She felt suddenly protective towards the young boy beside her. She, and Lovell, and all the other people present, knew, and faced the responsibilities of knowing, this precious secret. Now, she too was one of the elect.

"What did you thee?" asked Sidney.

"I saw the door closing," said Miriam. "That's all."

Across the table, Lovell smiled at her with approval. Her heart leapt, and Christmas Day became again the joyful festival she had always known.

❧

How sharply it came back, thought Miss Quinn, that memory of thirty years ago! The shock of her enlightenment was some measure of the joy she had formerly felt in the myth of Father Christmas. She was glad that Jenny and Robin were still ardent believers, and she must try and make sure that Hazel, on the brink of knowledge, did not suffer as she had done as a child, and did not tarnish the glitter for the younger ones.

Somewhere, in some distant copse, a fox gave an eerie cry.

The scudding clouds parted briefly, and a shaft of moonlight fell across the bed.

The night was made for sleeping, said Miriam to herself, and tomorrow there was much to be done. There were children to be tended, Eileen to visit, provisions to organize, and all to be accomplished amidst the joyous frenzy of Christmas Eve.

Resolutely, she applied herself to sleep.

Chapter 7

CHRISTMAS EVE

S HE AWOKE, much refreshed, still with the memories of past Christmas times about her, and determined to make the present one happy for the children.

It was still dark, but she could hear children's voices. Perhaps they were already dressed? She put her warm feet upon the chilly linoleum and went to the door. The house felt icy.

Sure enough, the two little girls were scampering about the long passage half-dressed. They greeted her with cries of joy, and bounced into her room unbidden. Wails from Robin could be heard in the distance.

"Oh, he's all right," said Hazel casually. "Daddy's put him on his potty, and he doesn't want to go. That's all."

Jenny was fingering Miriam's hairbrush.

"I've asked Father Christmas for one like this," she said.

Hazel's lip began to curl in a derisory manner, and Miriam, recalling her nighttime memory, put a hand on her arm. There was no mistaking the alert glance that the child flashed at her. She knew all right!

Remembering Lovell's meaning shake of the head so long ago, she repeated the small gesture to his daughter. The child half-smiled in return, squeezed the restraining hand upon her arm, and remained silent.

That, thought Miriam thankfully, was one hurdle surmounted!

"What do you have for breakfast?" she enquired, tactfully changing the subject.

"Cornflakes, or shredded wheat," said Hazel.

"Sometimes toast, if there's time," said Jenny.

"What does Daddy have?" asked Miriam, secretly thinking that Eileen should surely cook a breakfast, if not for the children, then for a man off to his parish duties in the coldest part of England.

"The same," they chorused.

"Go and get dressed," said Miriam, "and I'll make toast for us all, and perhaps a boiled egg."

"Oh, lovely!" squealed the children. "Let's go and tell Robin!"

They fled, leaving Miriam to have the bathroom in peace.

At breakfast, Miriam broached the practical problem of catering for the household for four days. The basic things seemed to be in the house, and she knew that there were Brussels sprouts, cabbages, and carrots in the vegetable garden.

A Christmas pudding stood on the pantry shelf, but she would have to make mince pies and other sweets, and where was the turkey — or was it to be a round of beef?

Lovell was vague. He rather thought a friend of theirs was supplying the turkey, but he would have imagined it should have been delivered by now.

"Will it be dressed?" asked Miriam, with considerable anxiety. She might be Sir Barnabas's right hand, but she knew her limits. Drawing a fowl was not among her talents.

"Dressed?" queried Hazel, egg spoon arrested halfway to her mouth. "What in?"

Gales of giggles greeted this sally.

"A bonnet," gasped Jenny, "and shawl! Like Jemima Puddleduck. That's what turkeys dress in!"

The two little girls rolled about in paroxysms of mirth. Lovell cast his eyes heavenward, in mock disdain.

"Dressed means ready to put in the oven," explained Miriam, laughing.

"I know a boy at school who can pull out the tubes and smelly bits," said Hazel, recovering slightly. "Is that what you mean?"

"Exactly," said Miriam.

At that moment the telephone rang, and Lovell vanished.

"It might still have its feathers on," remarked Jenny.

"And its head," added Hazel.

Miriam's qualms intensified.

"How do you get its head off?" enquired Jenny conversationally, scraping the last of her egg from the shell.

Miriam was spared replying as Lovell returned.

"The chairman of Eileen's bench. Just enquiring."

Eileen, she remembered now, had recently been made a magistrate. Frankly, she wondered if she were capable of the task, but simply said politely:

"Does she worry much about her duties?"

"What she really worries about," replied Lovell, "is whether she should wear a hat or not."

Then, sensing that this might smack of disloyalty, he enlarged on the many compliments he had heard from her fellows on the bench, on Eileen's good sense and fair-mindedness.

His discourse was cut short by a ring at the back door. Hazel skipped off to answer it and came back, much excited.

"It's the turkey man, Aunt Miriam, and it's all right! He's bare!"

Construing this correctly, Miriam felt a wave of

relief, and hurried to fetch the bird, Lovell following close behind to pay the bill.

A little later, she sallied forth with several baskets, and the three children in tow. Lovell had to conduct a funeral service and visit two desperately sick parishioners. He would be back to late lunch, and then stay at the vicarage while Miriam visited the hospital.

"Can you possibly get back by about four, do you think?" he enquired, consulting a list anxiously. "I'm supposed to call at the village hall to have tea with the Over-Sixty Club, and be at a Brownies' Carol Service in the next parish at the same time. Then I must have a word with the flower ladies, and get ready for the midnight service."

Miriam assured him that she could manage easily.

"Can we come and see Mummy? Can we?" clamored the girls. Miriam looked at Lovell.

"Sister made no objection last time, as long as they behave, of course, and aren't there too long. But how do you feel?"

"I'd like their company," said Miriam, and they fell upon her with shrieks of joy.

The grocer's shop was one of three in the village. Across the road was the butcher's, and next door was the post office which sold sweets and tobacco.

The proprietor of the village store bore a strong resemblance to Mrs. Pringle of Fairacre. She had the same square frame, the identical short-cropped hair, and an expression of malevolent resignation.

Fortunately, the similarity ended there, and she turned out to be unusually helpful about the needs of the vicarage household.

"Did you want the piece of gammon Mrs. Quinn asked about? I've put it by, in case."

"Yes, please," said Miriam. At least it would make a change from turkey in the days to come.

"And you'll want potatoes," Mrs. Bates informed her. "That half-hundredweight was nearly finished last week, Annie told me."

Miriam, slightly dazed, remembered that Eileen's mother's help was a local girl.

"I'm her auntie," vouchsafed Mrs. Bates, scrabbling in a box of potatoes hidden behind the counter. Fairacre all over again! thought Miriam.

"Take five pounds now, and my Bert'll bring up ten pounds tomorrow if that suits you. You don't want to hump all that lot, and Robin's push chair's not that strong."

Miriam agreed meekly. It was quite a change to be managed. Was this how Barney felt when she mapped out his routine?

With a shock she remembered that there had been no preparations made for lunch at home. For the first time in her life, she bought fish fingers, and a ready-made blackcurrant tart. How often she had watched scornfully the feckless mothers buying the expensive "convenience" foods. Now, with three children distracting her and the clock ticking on inexorably, she sympathized with them. Catering for one, she began to realize, was quite a different matter from trying to please the varying tastes of five people, and hungry ones at that.

"Where's Robin?" she enquired suddenly. The child had vanished.

Hazel and Jenny were talking to a boy in the door-way.

"Probably in the road," said Mrs. Bates. "And the traffic's something awful this morning."

There was a hint of mournful satisfaction in this remark that reminded Miriam yet again of the distant Mrs. Pringle.

She rushed to the door, heart thudding, calling his name. The road was clear, except for a scrawny dog carrying a large bone.

"It's all right!" shouted Mrs. Bates behind her. "He's here."

The child was sitting on the floor, hidden behind the end of the counter, beside a rolled-down sack containing dog biscuits which he was eating with the voracity of one just released from a concentration camp.

"Robin, *really!*" exclaimed his aunt. Like Tabitha Twitchit, she thought suddenly, I am affronted.

"Don't worry, miss. He's partial to dog biscuits. And these are extra pure," she added virtuously.

"You must let me pay you," said Miriam, hauling the child to his feet and brushing yellow sulphur biscuit crumbs from his coat.

"Oh, he's welcome," said Mrs. Bates indulgently. "I'll just add up the other."

By the time she had visited the butcher to buy steak and kidney for a casserole for the evening meal, and then the post office for stamps and sweets, Miriam seemed to have accumulated three heavy baskets.

The wind was now boisterous, and carrying rain bordering on sleet. The children did not seem to notice the cold, but Miriam, struggling with the erratic push chair and the shopping, felt frozen through.

Ah! Dear Holly Lodge! she thought with longing. Tucked into the shelter of the downs, screened by that stout hedge, when would she see it again?

🌿

"What a lovely, lovely lunch," sighed Jenny, leaning back replete.

"Excellent!" agreed her father.

Miriam was secretly amused. If her friends could have seen the meal she had assembled, fish fingers, instant potatoes, tinned beans, and bottled tomato sauce, followed by the bought fruit pie, her standing as a first-class cook would have taken a jolt.

And yet it had been relished. Perhaps there was a moral here, but there was certainly no time to pursue the thought, with the washing up to be done, the girls to get ready, and Robin to be put down for his afternoon nap. She must put the steak and kidney in a slow oven too, so that it could cook gently while they were at the hospital. How on earth did mothers manage? She was more exhausted now, at midday, than she was at the end of a hard week at the office.

At half-past two she set out, with the girls in a state of wild excitement in the back of the car. They were carrying their Christmas presents for Eileen, and keeping an eye on Miriam's. Tomorrow Lovell would be the only visitor at the hospital, while Miriam took charge at home.

Eileen looked prettier and younger than ever, propped against her pillows in a frilly pale blue nightgown. It so happened that Miriam's present was also a nightgown, but a black chiffon one

threaded with narrow black satin ribbon. It would make a splendid contrast, she thought, to the one she was now wearing.

Eileen greeted them all with hugs and kisses.

"You are a perfect angel to come to our rescue," she said when the little girls had been settled, in comparative peace, with some magazines. "Have you had a terrible time coping?"

Miriam reassured her.

"I think all the shopping's done. No doubt I've forgotten something quite vital like bread, but I've remembered stuffing for the bird and even salted peanuts in case people come in for drinks."

"That's more than I should have done," said Eileen cheerfully, and Miriam began to feel more drawn to her sister-in-law than ever before. There was something engaging about such candor.

"Is that lady dying?" asked Jenny, in a high carrying voice, her finger pointing to a gray-faced woman dozing in the next bed. Miriam went cold with shock.

Eileen laughed merrily.

"Good heavens, no! Mrs. White is getting better faster than any of us. Be very quiet, darling, so that she doesn't wake up."

At this point, Sister arrived, and asked Eileen if the children would like to see the Christmas tree in the children's ward. They departed happily.

"By the way," said Miriam, "did you know that Hazel has tumbled to Father Christmas?"

"Yes. I hope she won't tell Jenny yet."

Miriam explained what had happened.

"Always problems," said Eileen. "And with some you will be wrong whatever you do. I thought this when Lovell and I were invited out together, the other evening. He was suddenly taken ill. Of course I rang our hostess, and she said: 'Will you feel like coming?'

"What do you do? Say 'Yes' and be branded as callous to one's husband's sufferings, and probably greedy to boot, or say 'No' and let down the hostess?"

"Insoluble," agreed Miriam. "Or, worse still, wondering whether to pull the lavatory chain in the dead of night in someone else's house. If you do, you can imagine the startled hostess saying: 'You'd think she would have more sense than to rouse the whole household!' On the other hand, one is liable to be branded a perfect slut if the hostess visits the loo first in the morning!"

They laughed together, and Miriam, for the first time, felt completely at ease in Eileen's presence.

"But tell me about yourself," she said. "Are they getting things right?"

"I think so. They couldn't be kinder, and once the results of the tests are through I may be able to come

home. Strict diet, and all that, and weekly check-
ups, but I've a strong suspicion it won't come to surgery."

"Thank God for that!" said Miriam.

"You must be longing to get back to Fairacre," said
Eileen. "The vicarage is such a barn of a place. But
Lovell is terribly grateful to you for coming up so
quickly, and so am I, as you know. We should have
foundered without you. Ah, here comes Sister."

The children had been given a chocolate toy from
the tree, and were starry-eyed with pleasure.

"Shall I unwrap your presents while you're here?"
asked Eileen.

"Yes, yes. Do it now!" they clamored.

With great care, she undid the wrappings, read
the lopsided cards covered in kiss-crosses, and finally
displayed a canvas bookmark embroidered in lazy-
daisy stitch by Hazel and a thimble in a walnut-shell
case from Jenny.

"Perfect!" smiled Eileen, putting the thimble on
her finger, and the bookmark in the novel by her bed.
"Now Christmas has really begun!"

Miriam looked at her watch.

"I must take them back. Lovell has to be off again
by four. He'll be in tomorrow, and I'll come again
after that."

"Dear Miriam," murmured Eileen, as they kissed.
"No wonder Lovell adores you. You are an absolute
tower of strength."

Miriam called into Sister's room as they went out, to thank her for the children's presents, and to enquire after Eileen's progress.

"She's doing very well. We couldn't have a better patient, and a real help to the others in the ward."

"She says you are all very good to her."

"That's nothing to Mr. Quinn's kindness to my old mother," said Sister, with energy. "You don't forget help like that when you're in trouble. He lives by his beliefs, that brother of yours."

"He tries to, I know," replied Miriam, much moved.

"Come on, Aunt Miriam, we've got to get our things ready for Father Christmas," urged the girls.

"First things first," called Sister, as they left the hospital.

The wind had become a vicious howling gale by the time they reached home. The sleet slanted across the headlights, and a wicked draft blew from the east under the vicarage doors. Water was blowing onto the landing from a window which took the brunt of the weather, and Miriam searched for something to staunch the flow.

"Mummy just leaves it," said Jenny, faintly surprised at so much fuss over some intruding rain. "It always dries up after a bit."

Exhausted as she was, Miriam began to sympathize with this laissez faire attitude, although it was against all her principles. She rammed a shabby towel against the crack, and hoped for the best.

Lovell had departed into the waste of wind and water, and Robin's bath time arrived. Hazel and Jenny accompanied her to the bathroom, anxious to help and to explain to the boy the importance of hanging up his stocking.

Less hostile than the previous evening, nevertheless the child still resented Miriam's attentions.

"Dadda do!" he muttered sulkily. "Go away!"

"You're a bad boy," scolded Hazel, "to say that to Aunt Miriam when she's come all this way to look after you!"

Robin responded by blowing a mouthful of soapy water over his sister. Most of it went on Miriam's skirt.

Jenny improved the shining hour by telling the child about Father Christmas.

"And he'll creep into your room in a red coat," she began, but was interrupted by a fearful screeching from her brother.

"No want! No want!" he screamed, shaking his head violently.

Jenny looked resignedly at Miriam who was doing her best to soap his thrashing legs.

"You know, he's frightened, that's what! He's just *frightened* of Father Christmas. What'll we do?"

Hazel came to the rescue.

"Put his stocking on the banisters, then he'll be all right, won't he?"

She looked at Miriam with a conspiratorial glance.

"Good idea," said she hastily, praying that the secret would still be kept.

She hauled the boy out of the water, amidst more shrieking, and muffled his cries in a warm towel. The bathroom, steamy and damp, was the warmest place in the house, and she was loath to leave it to put the child into his cot in the chilly bedroom. What this place needs, she told herself, and will never get, is a thoroughly efficient central heating system.

The two little girls had climbed into the bath together, lured into an early bedtime by the promise of supper by the fire downstairs, and the happy prospect of hanging up stockings.

Miriam left them there while she warmed their milk in the kitchen. Outside, the rain lashed at the window, and the branches of the apple tree creaked and groaned. A particularly fierce draft under the larder door made a noise like a banshee wailing. This was Norfolk at its worst, thought Miriam, but at least the stove was warm, and the comforting smell of the steak casserole counteracted the bleakness outside.

The sitting room was snug with the curtains drawn and the fire blazing. The two little girls nursed their bowls of cornflakes liberally topped with brown sugar and raisins, and asked Miriam to tell them about Christmas when she was small.

"Well," began Miriam, "we used to hang up pillowcases, your Daddy and I."

"So do we. And stockings."

"And we left a mince pie and some milk for Father Christmas, in the hearth."

"So do we," they chorused.

"And after he'd been," said Miriam, looking squarely at Hazel, whose face remained rapt, "we took our pillowcases into grandma and grandpa's bed and undid all our parcels."

"And what did you have?"

Miriam suddenly remembered the agonizing night when she felt her parcels as the tears rolled down her cheeks. She could taste them now, salty and bitter, and feel the lump in her aching throat.

"Are you all right?" asked Hazel.

"Yes, just thinking," said Miriam. "Oh, a doll, and a tea set with little flowers on it, and, of course, a tangerine and nuts and sweets. Lots of lovely things." And heartbreak, she added silently. God, that heartbreak! Nothing had ever hurt so since!

"Can we bring our things into your bedroom?" asked Jenny, spooning up the last drop.

"Of course you can!" cried Miriam. "On Christmas Day you can do anything you like! Within reason," she added prudently.

They skipped upstairs before her, and accompanied her to the linen cupboard for two pillowcases. A pair of Eileen's stockings already hung over their bed rail.

"Do you think they'll be full?" asked Jenny.

"Positively brimming over," Miriam promised her, tucking them in, and praying that sleep would soon engulf them.

Later that evening, she and Lovell drowsed before the fire, before he went over to the church for his late service.

In her lap billowed the great black mass of Lovell's cassock.

"Must have caught my heel in the hem," he said apologetically, as he handed it over. "Do you mind?"

She now stitched languidly, thinking yet again how many varied tasks fell to the lot of a married woman.

"I wish I could have found someone else to do it — and to help you in the house," said Lovell. "But everyone's so busy at Christmas time. Looking back, I realize how lucky we were at home to have dear old Euphrosyne and her like, coping in the kitchen. It meant mother had the energy needed to cope with parish affairs."

"From what I hear," said Miriam, snipping black cotton, "Eileen does very well."

"She has to do far too much," sighed Lovell. "How did she look today?"

"Ravishing as ever," said Miriam, and told him about her visit, and Sister's kindness, and her remark about his own.

Lovell looked surprised.

"Really? I did nothing you know. Just called now and again."

"And she also said that Eileen was a marvelous patient and a great help in the ward."

His face softened.

"She's the bravest person I know. She's been so sweet with that poor woman in the next bed. A terminal case, they call it. She wasn't expected to live through the night."

Miriam remembered her niece's query, her own horror, and Eileen's courageous laughter. There was certainly more to this sister-in-law of hers than she had ever imagined.

"Well, there you are," she said, shaking out the cassock. "I shall wait up for you, and we'll have the fun of filling the pillowcases together."

"You shouldn't. You look whacked, so don't stay up just for me."

He shrugged into the cassock, threw his coat over his shoulders and made for the door.

"I shall be back soon after midnight," he shouted above the wind, waved, and was gone.

Miriam was about to return to the fireside when she remembered that she had intended to stuff the turkey and prepare some of the vegetables for the morrow.

Should she go into the kitchen and tackle these chores? Or should she give way to temptation and collapse into the arm chair?

Bravely, she made her way towards the larder, followed by Copper, ever-anxious for a meal.

"And to think," she told the dog, "that I'm known as a working woman. I wonder what Eileen is?"

Chapter 8

CHRISTMAS DAY

THE DAY BEGAN, in pitch darkness, at five-thirty.
Miriam's door opened, and Hazel and
Jenny entered dragging their spoils behind them.

"You said we could come," beamed Hazel.

"And you said we could do anything we liked on
Christmas Day, so here we are!"

Miriam sat up and switched on the bedside lamp.
Her head was heavy with sleep, her eyes felt as
though they were full of biscuit crumbs. But this
was Christmas morning, and although it had come
far too soon for comfort, then Christian feelings
must predominate.

"Happy Christmas, darlings," she said, between
yawns. "Switch on the electric fire, Hazel, and both
come into bed. You must be frozen."

They joyously flung their laden pillowcases onto
their aunt's stomach, partially winding her. Their
bare feet were like four ice-blocks pressed against
her own warm legs. Their hands, diving for their
treasures, were mottled with the cold.

"Where's Robin?" asked Miriam.

"Still asleep. So's Daddy. Shall we go and fetch them?"

"No, no. They'll come along later. Let's see all these gorgeous things."

She duly admired books, jigsaw puzzles, and a complicated board game which she feared would be beyond her when the time came for it to be played.

There were recorders, played with more enthusiasm than harmony, dolls and their clothes — remarkably sophisticated to Miriam's eye. No doll of hers ever had ski clothes, bathing dresses, or evening cloaks. These beauties even had handbags to match their different outfits. The girls were enchanted.

Miriam had given Hazel a toy sewing machine, and Jenny a little cooking stove. She was relieved to see how ecstatically these were received, and promised to help them when they started to use them.

"I shall make tiny, tiny, dear little chips and fry them in this frying pan," cried Jenny. "You can have some for supper."

Miriam lay back on her pillow and watched them affectionately. Everything enchanted them, even the two plain aprons sent by a distant great-aunt. It was good to see such unspoilt children. Lovell and Eileen had done a good job with these two, thought their aunt proudly.

She looked about the room, which was now beginning to get warm. The children had hung a red paper bell over the door when they had decorated the house with all the Christmas paper chains, folding fans, and other ornaments earlier in the week. It really looked rather pretty, thought Miriam, remembering how she and Lovell had always adored unfolding these showy decorations as children to deck the old Fenland vicarage. What would these children think of her own bare quarters at Holly Lodge, if they could see them?

But something indefinable was missing. Was it the smell of tangerines?

Before she could pin it down, Lovell came in carrying Robin with his stocking.

"Merry Christmas!" they all shouted.

"It's marvelously warm in here," said Lovell. "Reminds me of Christmas morning at home when we used to have the Valor Perfection stove alight in the bedroom."

"That's it!" cried Miriam. "I've been missing the smell of paraffin!"

"And a good thing too, I should think," said Lovell, helping his youngest to unwrap a furry panda.

"But it was heavenly in the dark," remembered Miriam, "making lovely patterns on the ceiling."

"And lovely smuts when it smoked," added Lovell.

The little girls were busily opening their brother's presents and urging him to admire them. Robin appeared to be as sleepy as Miriam felt herself, and greeted each discovery with a marked lack of enthusiasm.

"What we need," said Miriam, when the last parcel was undone and the bedroom floor was awash with Christmas wrappings, "is an early breakfast. And then you can play with your new toys before we go to church."

Lovell had a service at eight, and Miriam proposed to take the children to the eleven o'clock service, bringing them out before the sermon.

"But you can't leave the *turkey*," protested Hazel, as though it were an invalid aunt in need of constant care.

"I can, you know," said Miriam. "You'll see."

"I could cook something on my stove," said Jenny. "Peas, say."

"There'd only be a mouthful," said Hazel.

"I could *keep on* cooking peas!" replied Jenny snappily. "Then there'd be enough. Fish shops *keep on cooking*, don't they, Aunt Miriam? Everyone has enough."

By mid-morning tempers were beginning to fray. After such an early awakening, and now that the toys had been inspected, the children started to quarrel.

It was the first time that Miriam had seen the two sisters at war, and she was staggered at the ferocity of the battle. She was at a loss, too, to know how best to quell this uprising.

Robin, more animated than he had yet appeared, looked on the scene with approval, clapping his hands as Jenny clutched her sister's long hair and attempted to haul it from her scalp.

Hazel retaliated with a resounding smack on Jenny's cheek. Screams rent the air, and Miriam rushed to part them. This was something entirely new to her. Once, she remembered, she had been called to a couple in the typing room at the office who had reduced each other to tears over some business about a boyfriend. That had been bad enough, but this was real commando stuff.

A sharp scratch from Hazel's finger nail caused

her such sudden pain that involuntarily she smacked the child's arm, and Jenny's too. The maneuver worked like a charm, both fell apart, open-mouthed with astonishment.

"Mummy *never*, *never* hits us," exclaimed Hazel, much shocked.

"Nor Daddy," cried Jenny, coming to her late enemy's support.

The words: "More fool them," hovered on Miriam's lips, but she forbore to utter them. She was still suffering from pain, shock, and some shame at the violence of her reaction.

"You can go upstairs, and get ready for church," she said instead. "And no more nonsense!"

They went out quietly, but before they had reached the stairs Miriam heard them giggling together, all conflict over.

An ominous pattering noise attracted her attention. Robin was inspecting a growing puddle on the kitchen floor.

"Good boy!" he said approvingly. "Good boy, Robin."

Sighing, Miriam went in search of a bucket and floor cloth.

An hour later, she and her charges sat decorously in church awaiting Lovell's entrance.

The building was plain, with only a few mural tab-

lets bearing testimony to the virtues of the deceased
and the grief of those mourning them. A threadbare
banner hung from one wall, a reminder of the gal-
lantry of an East Anglian regiment and

> *Old unhappy far-off things*
> *And battles long ago.*

The church was half-full, which Miriam rightly
construed as a good congregation. She had attended
a service here on one occasion with only three other
worshipers.

The organ swelled into a recognizable tune, and
the congregation rose as the choir entered, followed
by Lovell.

"That's my Daddy!" cried Robin joyously, much
to the delight of nearby worshipers. Jenny and
Hazel shook their heads with disapproval, but were
obviously secretly proud of their brother's intelligence.

The service began, but its measured beauty failed
to hold Miriam's attention, distracted as she was by
having to find the place for the two little girls and by
restraining Robin, who was busy licking the var-
nished pew shelf as though it were made of butter-
scotch, which it somewhat resembled.

This activity was accompanied by loud smacking
noises and an appreciative growling, such as puppies
make when enjoying a bone. Miriam's effort to

divert him were met with vociferous resistance and
a renewed attack upon the woodwork. A particularly solemn silence, at the end of one of the prayers,
was broken by a crunching sound. Robin, raising his
head to admire his toothwork, turned, dribbling
heavily, to Miriam, and patted the wet shelf encour-
agingly.

"Auntie bite!" he demanded. "Auntie bite too!"

"No!" hissed Miriam fiercely. Really, to think
that a two-year-old could cause so much embarrass-
ment! She was conscious of considerable merriment
in the pews behind her. Should she take the child
out, she wondered?

Luckily, at this juncture they all stood for the
hymn preceding the sermon.

"Do we put our money in now?" enquired Hazel
loudly. "Because I've lost mine."

Jenny, with sisterly concern, fell to the floor and
began searching busily along a very dusty heating
pipe.

"P'raps it's rolled under the seat," she suggested,
pointing with a black hand. Hazel bent down, as
though about to join her in the depths.

"Leave it," begged Miriam helplessly. "I will give
you some more."

"But we *can't* just leave it!" protested Jenny. By
now her face was striped with grime. She looked like
a very cross tiger cub.

"It's not now anyway," responded Hazel. "It's the next hymn we put the money in. Daddy does his talking, and then we put it in, don't we, Aunt Miriam?"

"Well, we won't be here then," argued Jenny, "so what shall we do with our money? Aunt Miriam, we don't want any collection money, so can we keep it?"

Powerless to check this flow of conversation, Miriam saw, with infinite relief, that Lovell was ascending the stairs to the pulpit. This was her cue to remove his lively offspring.

She began to usher the children into the aisle. Fortunately, she had purposely taken a pew near to the door. Robin resisted strongly, and appealed to the distant figure in the pulpit.

"Dadda!" he screamed lustily. "Dadda do! Dadda do!"

The two little girls contented themselves with waving cheerfully as they made for the door, but Robin sat suddenly in the aisle and refused to budge.

An elderly sidesman, seeing Miriam's dilemma, advanced and picked up the boy, who made himself as stiff as a board, whilst keeping up a barrage of ear-splitting yells.

He was borne towards the door, Miriam following. She gave one apologetic backward glance towards Lovell. His dark face was impassive, but there was a gleam in his eye which told her clearly of his enjoyment of the scene.

"Like a sweet?" said the sidesman to Robin, when
they gained the porch. The screams stopped abruptly.

He deposited the boy on the gravel path outside
and felt in his waistcoat pocket. Hazel and Jenny
watched with attention.

He produced three small fruit drops each wrapped
in cellophane, and handed them down.

"Always as well to have sweets on you when there
are children around," he said kindly to Miriam, and
departed before she had time to thank him properly.

It was wonderful to be out in the air again. The
wind was still strong, but the rain had gone, and now

the scudding clouds parted, and the sun lit up the wide Norfolk fields around the flint church.

"I *love* Christmas!" said Jenny, cheek bulging. "Do you?"

Miriam looked at the three children, so quickly transformed into angels.

"Yes," she said. "I do."

🌿

The turkey, which had been left to its own devices in the oven much to the concern of the two little girls, had assumed a luscious golden brown when Miriam returned to baste it.

She put on the vegetables and topped up the water in the steamer holding the Christmas pudding before going to set the table.

She had ransacked the airing cupboard and at last found a large white damask cloth, old and beautifully starched, with several darns executed, she guessed, by a long-dead hand. No one these days, surely, could be bothered to do such fine work.

Spread upon the dining room table and decorated with two candlesticks borrowed from the mantelpiece, it began to look more like a festive board, although Miriam cursed herself for forgetting to buy crackers, those instant decorations. As it was, there was no time to search for flowers or ribbons, but she filched a few holly sprigs from above the pictures where the children had put them, and set them round the candlesticks.

"It's *marvelous!*" cried Hazel.

"Can we put some pretty things too?" queried Jenny.

"Yes, do," said Miriam, rushing to the kitchen to attend to an ominous hissing noise.

When she returned, she found that Hazel had added a small sleigh holding Father Christmas and bath cubes, an inspired present from an aunt in America, whilst Jenny had purloined the fairy from the top of the Christmas tree to add to the scene.

Robin's contribution was a toy camel with three lead legs and one of plasticine. It added an exotic touch as it leaned, in a drunken fashion against a candlestick.

Lovell admired everything warmly when he returned from church, and the meal was as cheerful as he and Miriam could make it for the children.

Afterwards, the two adults dozed while Robin slept upstairs and the two little girls played with their new toys. A walk was planned for three o'clock, but when the time came Miriam saw that Lovell was still deep in sleep. Now she observed how tired he looked, how the lines had deepened in his face and how his dark hair was showing flecks of gray. His work and Eileen's illness were taking their toll of his energy, and she grieved for him.

Quietly, she slipped from the room and summoned Hazel and Jenny. A look into Robin's room showed the boy as deep in slumber as his father.

"We'll play games at the end of the garden," said Miriam, "instead of going for a walk. Then we can be near Robin if he wakes."

"Goody-goody-gum-drops!" cried Jenny. "We'll have longer with our toys then."

The kitchen garden was a vast area with a mellowed brick and flint wall. A hundred years or so earlier it must have been the pride of a head gardener and probably two or three undergardeners. Now it sheltered only a few rows of Brussels sprouts, carrots, and parsnips, but it afforded a playground out of the wind and far enough away from the house for the children's shouts to be unheard.

Miriam showed them how to play two-ball against the wall, and was surprised and proud to find that she had not lost her skill over the years. After initial difficulties, the girls soon became quite dexterous, the only snag being that only two balls could be found, and they had to take it in turns.

"As soon as the shops open," promised Miriam, "I'll buy you two new ones each."

"But that's not till Monday," wailed Hazel. "It's ages away!"

" 'What can't be cured must be endured,' " Miriam said cheerfully, quoting Euphrosyne.

"I don't understand that," said Jenny flatly.

"It means you have to lump it!" her sister told her, appropriating the balls briskly.

🌿

The menfolk were much refreshed after their naps, and over tea Lovell spoke of the Boxing Day meet which was always held in the square of the local market town.

"Shall we all go?" he asked.

"Yes, yes!" chorused the children. "All in one car! All squashed up and cosy. And take our presents so we can play while we wait!"

Lovell looked at Miriam. She thought quickly. Certainly lunch would be cold turkey, and that presented no difficulties, but she longed to attack some of the more urgent cleaning that had obviously been neglected since Eileen's departure. She did not want Lovell to see her scrubbing his kitchen floor, but that is what she had planned to do if she could manage it unobserved. Then there was the gammon to cook, and a vast amount of necessary sweeping and dusting to do. To have two hours alone would suit her plans perfectly.

"I think I'll stay here, if you don't mind," she replied. "There are several things to do, and I really ought to ring Joan. I shall probably catch her in the morning."

"Of course, of course," said Lovell. He spoke sympathetically. To his eyes, the girl looked absolutely exhausted and he felt horribly guilty. She worked hard at the office, had undertaken a long journey, and was coping superbly with his family. Obviously, it would do her good to have a brief time on her own.

"I'll take the brood off soon after ten," he promised. "The meet is at eleven, and we'll be back before one o'clock."

"Marvelous!" said Miriam, with relief.

The rest of the day passed quietly. Lovell went to the hospital alone to see Eileen, and the children, tired after all the excitement, were docile enough to go to bed early.

Miriam put the gammon to boil, averted her eyes from the state of the kitchen floor, and fell, bone-weary, into an armchair.

A vision of Holly Lodge as it would be in the New Year, if she ever returned to her ministrations there, floated before her. Quiet, warm, clean — a haven of solitude and silence — it hung before her mind's eye as beautiful as a jewel.

She sighed, and slept.

Chapter 9

BOXING DAY

*I*T WAS OVERCAST when Miriam awoke next morning. From her bedroom window she looked out across the flat countryside towards the sea, some twenty miles away.

Inky-dark clouds were moving in slowly, dwarfing the trees and farmsteads with menacing stature. Already, a boisterous wind was blowing, and Miriam predicted storms before long. She only hoped that the rain would hold off long enough for the family to enjoy the meet.

They all drove off in high spirits, and Miriam returned from waving goodbye to tackle the worst of the mess.

She tidied the larder, ruthlessly throwing away the flotsam and jetsam of the past week: stale bread, ancient scraps of cheese, decaying and unidentifiable morsels on saucers, withered apples, and the like. The birds descended in a flock, sea gulls among the more usual visitors, and snapped up this bounty.

She scrubbed the sink and draining boards, thankful that, with all its drawbacks, the vicarage was blessed with plenty of hot water.

There was something rather satisfying, she found, in scrubbing the tiles of the kitchen floor. The clean, sweet-smelling wetness, which grew as she retreated backwards from it on her knees, delighted her, and although she doubted if anyone would ever notice the result of her labors, she was content with her small reward of a job well done.

That finished, she mounted the steep stairs, man-handling the vacuum sweeper and dusters, and set about the bedrooms. The chaos of the girls' room was daunting, and the fact that the dirty linen basket was overflowing was another reminder of work ahead. Really, thought Miriam, dusting vigorously, I should never have made a wife and mother! Looking after Barney from nine till five is more than enough for me!

By twelve-thirty the house looked reasonably tidy, and she skinned the gammon, gave up a fruitless search for breadcrumbs with which to adorn it, and set the table. It was while she was doing this that she heard the car return, and voices in the hall.

She emerged from the kitchen to find that Lovell was accompanied by another man.

Who could this stranger be? She looked again, and hurried forward smiling.

"Why, Martin, how lovely to see you again!"

🌿

"Brought him back from the meet for a drink," said Lovell beaming. "It must be nearly a year since we met."

"And more like ten since I saw Miriam," said Martin. "And as elegant as ever."

They moved into the sitting room, the children following.

"You run and play in the garden for a few minutes," directed Lovell.

"But we're hungry!"

"When is lunch ready?"

"Can't we have a drink too?"

The protests came thick and fast.

"Have an apple each," suggested Miriam diplomatically, "and go and practice two-ball."

This solution pleased all, and the adults were left to sip their sherry in peace.

It appeared that Martin Farrar's farm lay some twelve miles on the other side of the market town.

"Corn mainly, and sugar beets," he told Miriam, "though I keep a few head of cattle. I'm hoping to have pigs some day too. But tell me your news. Where do you live now?"

Miriam told him about the job in Caxley and her new home at Holly Lodge. She found herself rattling away — Martin had always been a good listener, she remembered — and was about to enlarge on her interrupted decorating of the sitting room when she remembered Lovell's feelings, and checked herself.

"I stopped in Cambridge on the journey up," she said instead, and that opened the way to a flood of happy reminiscences.

"You'll stay to lunch, won't you?" said Lovell. He turned to Miriam anxiously. "It is all right? It's cold turkey, I believe?"

"Quite right. And gammon too. And it will be lovely if you can stop."

"I'd love to," said Martin.

Miriam retired to the kitchen to finish her preparations. She was slightly puzzled. What about Martin's wife? Would she be waiting lunch for him? No mention had been made of her. Perhaps she was away. But, at Christmas time? Had they parted?

Perplexed, she assembled pickles and an unopened giant-size packet of potato crisps. She put in the oven the batch of mince pies she had made earlier, and hoped that the cheese board would provide for any empty corners left by the lunch she had prepared.

The children ate hungrily, their appetites whetted by the fresh air. As they ate, the first of the raindrops spattered against the window and the wind began to roar more loudly.

"We're in for it, I'm afraid," said Martin. "The glass was going back this morning. As long as we don't get snow, I don't mind."

"Do you remember the winter of 1962 and 1963?" asked Lovell. "My parents were marooned in the vicarage for four weeks, with eight-foot drifts cutting them off. Thank God, my mother always did a lot of bottling and preserving. Father said he hoped never to face another bottled gooseberry in his lifetime!"

"We were just married," said Martin, "and had misjudged the fuel amounts. Binnie walked about clutching a hot-water bottle all day. It taught us to stock up properly another time."

"I was in London," said Miriam, "a bitter waste

of brown slush everywhere. Town snow is so much worse than country snow."

After lunch, the little girls elected to paint at the kitchen table and Miriam left them to enjoy the new paints and painting books while she put Robin to bed, and Lovell made coffee.

The rain now lashed the house, and Miriam stuffed the towel again into the vulnerable landing window before going downstairs to the fireside.

Martin was helping himself to Lovell's brew and surveying the weather.

"I ought to be getting back pretty soon. I'm the cattleman this afternoon, and it's going to get dark early today."

They sat at peace, enjoying the warmth of the fire and their coffee.

Miriam looked at Martin as he gazed somnolently at the blazing logs. He had worn well. His hair was thick, his face tanned with his outdoor life, and he was as lean as he had always been. And yet, there was an air of unhappiness about him. Perhaps he felt the same about herself. Perhaps it was simply the passing of the years, the change from the effervescence of youth to the sobriety of middle age.

Middle age! It was a shock to realize that she was half-way to her three-score years and ten. Martin must be nearing forty.

He put his cup down in the hearth with a clatter, and stretched luxuriously.

"Oh, if I could only stay by this fire! Instead, I must go back and bash swedes."

"Do you really bash swedes?" asked Miriam.

"Not today," said Martin, with a laugh. "Just feed the cattle with something less demanding."

He held out his hand.

"Thank you for giving me lunch, and for your company. I come your way about twice a year. Perhaps I may call in, now I know where you live?"

"I shall look forward to it."

"Well, it may be in a few weeks' time. There's a cattle dealer in Wales I want to see."

He made his farewells, and they watched him race through the rain to his Land-Rover. The rain was now torrential, and the branches clashed overhead in the force of the gale, but Martin's grin was cheerful as he waved goodbye.

"Nice to see him again," said Lovell as they shut the door against the weather. "We live so near, really, and were such close friends in the old days, it seems absurd to lose touch as we have done."

The fireside was doubly snug after their brush with the weather outside. Peace reigned in the kitchen, and Robin slept aloft. Miriam and Lovell resumed their seats with relief.

She lay back, musing about the encounter. It was good to see Martin again. Their early flirtation had been a happy one, and it was comforting to see, once again, the unfeigned affection and admiration in his

looks. She hoped she would see him again when he
traveled to Wales next.

"What is Martin's wife like?" she asked.

"Martin's wife?" Lovell looked startled.

"Binnie, he called her," said Miriam.

Lovell shook his head sadly.

"Poor Binnie! I should have remembered that
you knew nothing about it. She died two years ago
— quite that, longer perhaps. I can't quite remember."

"How ghastly for Martin! What was it?"

"One of those incredibly stupid accidents that

strain one's religious beliefs sorely. She was bathing within a few yards of the shore, when a freak wave carried her out to sea, and a sort of whirlpool sucked her under. There were treacherous currents there always, we heard later."

"Was Martin there?"

"He had gone to fetch towels from the car, and returned to find the rescue operation going on. The ghastly thing was that the body wasn't washed up until the next tide."

"Poor Martin! And no children?"

"There was one on the way, which made it worse, of course. I heard that Martin was in an appalling state of shock for months. His old mother was a tower of strength, and went to live at the farm with him."

"I remember her," replied Miriam, recalling the ramrod figure of Mrs. Farrar, her white hair and her deep voice. "Dreadful for her too."

"Anyway," said Lovell, "he seems to have recovered, and let's hope he finds someone else one day."

"That's Robin," exclaimed Miriam, at the sound of a distant wailing.

And she went to resume her duties.

She traveled alone to see Eileen that evening, Lovell volunteering to see his family into bed.

As she drove through the roaring night, buffeted by a fierce northeaster, she suddenly remembered that she had forgotten to telephone Joan. Martin's arrival had put it out of her head.

Lovell's account of Martin's tragedy had moved her deeply. Why did these things have to happen? Lovell's comment about the strain on one's religious beliefs, in the face of such senseless horror, was understandable. If he, so secure and ardent in his faith, could feel thus, how easy it was to forgive weaker souls who turned against their religion in such circumstances. Martin appeared to have weathered his own storm remarkably well. Possibly the fact that his work must go on in rain or shine had helped him through the worst. She was glad she knew about it, if she were to see him in the future. When she had said that she would look forward to seeing him again, she had spoken from her heart.

Eileen was wearing the new black nightgown, and looked prettier than ever. She was in good spirits.

"I ought to know, very soon, if I'm coming home next week," she told Miriam. "How I long for it! Tell me, how are you managing?"

Miriam told her the scraps of news, how helpful the children had been, how she had introduced them to two-ball, how beautiful the church had looked decked for Christmas, and, finally, how Lovell had brought Martin to lunch.

Eileen's face lit up.

"I'm so glad! We feel so terribly sorry for him, and we wish we saw more of him. He ought to marry again. He's such a dear."

She looked at Miriam with such an openly speculative eye that it was impossible not to laugh. Eileen laughed too, with such infectious gaiety that the woman in the next bed said:

"She's as good as a tonic is Mrs. Quinn!"

And it was then that Miriam suddenly realized that there was a new neighbor. Mrs. White, of the gray sad countenance, had gone, it seemed, to a colder bed under the Norfolk sky.

"I'm not really matchmaking," said Eileen lightly.

"I should hope not," replied Miriam. "Tell me, how did Christmas Day go in here?"

Eileen was willing to be deflected from the subject of Martin, much to Miriam's relief, and launched into a spirited account of the chief surgeon's prowess in turkey-carving, the morning carols, and the visit of the Mayor and his retinue.

Miriam stayed later than she intended, reveling in Eileen's racy descriptions, and the undoubted fact that she seemed stronger and more relaxed after her few days in hospital.

"You'll have Annie back on Monday," said Eileen, as they said goodbye. "And with any luck, I'll be home very soon after."

"We'll have a grand celebration," promised Miriam, fastening her coat, before leaving the warmth of the ward to face the gales outside.

Chapter 10

GOING HOME

*T*HE WEEKEND passed remarkably peacefully. Miriam felt more confident now that she was becoming accustomed to the routine of the household. One great blessing was that all the family seemed to eat most of the things she put before them, although turkey in a mild cheese sauce was greeted by Jenny with the remark that she "didn't like white gravy." However, her helping vanished, assisted, no doubt, by Hazel's offer to eat her share.

The craze for two-ball persisted, and the two little girls spent any rain-free periods — which were few — bouncing and catching the balls against the wall of the kitchen garden, twirling and clapping as Miriam had shown them.

It seemed a good idea to drive into the market town on Saturday morning, in the hope that a toy shop would be open. They were lucky enough to find a sports shop doing a brisk trade with two girls buying skiing equipment and a scoutmaster buying camping stoves. A basket of rubber balls, red, blue, yellow, and green, drew Hazel and Jenny like a magnet, and they ended by selecting two red and two green.

"I think you should have three each," said Miriam. "You ought to have a spare in case one gets lost."

"But can you afford it?" asked Hazel anxiously. "After Christmas too?"

"I think so," said Miriam.

"But you haven't got a husband to give you any money like Mummy," protested Jenny. "Are you sure?"

"I go to work, you know, so I earn some money."

"A lot? A pound a week?"

"A little more than that," admitted Miriam.

The girls sighed with relief.

"Then you're quite rich, aren't you?" smiled Hazel.

"Well then, thank you very much," said Jenny, choosing a yellow one for her spare ball. "You are kind, as well as rich."

The baker's shop was open next door, and Miriam bought fresh currant buns for tea, and a veal and ham pie as a change from the turkey.

"You must be *really* rich," observed Hazel, as they climbed into the car with their purchases, "if you can buy a great big pie like that. Mummy always makes ours, because she says they are so dear in the shops."

"Well, this is a treat," explained Miriam. And a

time- and energy-saver for a struggling aunt, she added to herself.

🌿

She found time to ring Joan who sounded busy and happy.

"Roger goes tomorrow. A friend is picking him up and they are flying to Switzerland at six o'clock. Plenty of snow there, they say."

"None at Fairacre, I hope?"

"Not yet, but it's cold enough."

They exchanged news. Barbara and the family were off on the Monday. And when could Joan hope to see Miriam?

"With luck, during next week," said Miriam. "It depends if Eileen is allowed home, and how strong she feels."

"Well, Holly Lodge is waiting for you," said Joan. "So come as soon as you can."

"I can promise that," Miriam assured her.

🌿

The gales continued, rising to their height on Sunday night. There were tales of fishing boats smashed at their moorings, and of large ships riding out the storm within sight of the Norfolk coast. At places the sea had flooded the marshland, and great damage was reported from the seaside towns on the Norfolk and Suffolk coasts. Men spent the weekend filling sandbags to block the gaps in the sea wall where the violence of the high tide had breached it.

At the vicarage, some tiles were blown from the roof and an ancient apple tree was toppled, its roots exposed to the children's horrified gaze and its branches enmeshing a chicken house, mercifully empty.

For the first time, Miriam saw the children frightened that night. The house shuddered in the onslaught, and the banshee wailings, which Miriam had thought belonged to the kitchen only, were increased to envelop the upstairs corridors.

Miriam left a night-light burning in a saucer of water to comfort the little girls. The tall shadows, made by the brave little light, took her back in an instant to her own childhood in just such a bleak vicarage, and she kissed the little girls with extra warmth and sympathy.

The nine o'clock news was devoted largely to the havoc caused by the storm, related with the usual zest with which the imparting of bad news is passed on. Shades of Mrs. Pringle, thought Miriam, watching a woman smugly explaining how she had found her neighbor pinned beneath her own coal shed and describing, with relish, the extent of her injuries.

"That's enough of that!" said Lovell, switching it

off. "If I know anything about it, it will have blown itself out within twenty-four hours."

🦋

It was at twelve the next day when the telephone rang, and it was Eileen on the line, sounding highly jubilant.

"It looks as though I can come home tomorrow. Isn't it wonderful? Can Lovell fetch me in the afternoon? The doctor wants to see me in the morning, and it's really simpler if I have lunch here."

"Marvelous!" cried Miriam. "Let me call Lovell. He's in the garden, sawing the apple tree into logs."

"Any damage?"

"Very little," Miriam told her, "and the wind is dying down nicely."

"Look out for floods by the river," warned Eileen. "The papers haven't arrived yet, and they say a lot of people have had to leave their houses in the low-lying part of the town. Poor things! Can you imagine anything worse than finding your carpets floating downstairs?"

"Yes. Floating upstairs. Here's Lovell now," called Miriam, handing over the telephone to her wind-blown brother.

She could hear the excitement in his voice as she returned to the mound of washing which she was tackling. With any luck, she thought, it would be dry and ironed before the mistress of the house returned. And tomorrow morning, she must go foraging for food again.

That afternoon, when she and the children returned from a windy walk, they found Annie on the doorstep. The children rushed to greet her. Robin put his arms up around her waist and kissed the fourth button of her raincoat rapturously.

"How lovely to see you," cried Miriam. "Come in, and tell me what you usually do."

"Well," said Annie, "I help to get tea, and then I bathe Robin, and then I do anything Mrs. Quinn wants — ironing usually, or a bit of mending — and then I help put Jenny and Hazel to bed, and then I go home."

She was a thick-set cheerful girl with long straight hair tied in a pony tail and the brightest dark eyes that Miriam had ever seen.

"That sounds wonderful," said Miriam. "Let's get tea together now, and I'll start the ironing while you put Robin to bed later on."

"And my mum said, as it's school holidays and Mrs. Quinn's been took bad, I can come most of the day, just when it helps. I could do shopping and that, and take the children out for their walk. Just what's best."

"You are an angel," said Miriam fervently. "I'll

speak to Mr. Quinn when he comes in, and we'll arrange something."

Tea was taken at the kitchen table, and Miriam could see how competent and calm the young girl was with her charges, and how much they adored her. It was a noisy meal, with constant interruptions to fetch new toys to be admired. No doubt about it, thought Miriam, Annie was a treasure.

Miriam heard Lovell come in, and hurried into the sitting-room to tell him the good news.

"God bless Annie!" he said sincerely. "For this week, anyway, it would seem perfect if she came, say, at eleven and had coffee with us, and stayed the rest of the day, up till the children's bedtime, if her mother is agreeable."

"Go and have a word with her," suggested Miriam.

And so, to everyone's relief and joy, matters were arranged.

Annie's addition to the household was certainly a blessing, as Miriam soon discovered. By the time she arrived on Tuesday morning, Miriam had put Eileen and Lovell's bedroom to rights, had changed sheets, put out fresh soap and towels, and even found a few sprigs of yellow winter jasmine to put in a little vase by Eileen's bed.

Annie departed towards the village after her coffee, with a long shopping list, three baskets, and the children. Copper too decided to accompany them, and for the first time Miriam found herself the only living thing in the house, for Lovell was out visiting sick parishioners.

It was bliss to have the kitchen to herself, and to be able to follow a train of thought without urgent infant demands for attention. She prepared lunch, and even made a large batch of shortbread which, with any luck, could be stored in a tin for future use when she herself had gone back to Fairacre.

She had purposely made no firm plans for her return. It all depended on Eileen, but secretly she longed to get back within the next few days to finish her sitting room and to be ready for the office on the following Monday.

Her meditations were soon interrupted by the return of Annie and her charges, and the necessity of storing away shopping and setting the table for lunch.

"Why can't we go with Daddy to fetch Mummy?" complained Hazel.

"Because it will be much nicer to get things ready for her here," said Miriam firmly. "You can put a hot bottle in her bed in case she feels tired, and Jenny can get the tea tray ready."

They looked doubtful about these arrangements but fell in with the plans without argument. On such a joyous occasion, fighting seemed out of place.

As if to add to the general air of festivity, the sun
had come out, and the wind was less violent, although strong enough to send great galleons of white
clouds scudding across the blue sky. On the wide
Norfolk fields below, the shadows chased each other
across hedges and ditches, so that the countryside
was alternately lit with golden sunshine and deepest
shadow. The change in weather brought a refresh-
ment of spirit, and when at last Lovell's car drew up
at the front door and Eileen emerged with arms out-
stretched, the family burst from the front door with
cries of excitement.

"Do you want to go to bed?" demanded Hazel, when their mother was at last sitting by the fire.

"Heavens, no!" cried Eileen. "Why?"

"Because I've put in a bottle for you."

"That's very kind, but it will do beautifully for later on."

"Have some tea," urged Jenny, anxious to display her preparations.

"Not at three, darling," said her mother. "Just let me sit and look at you all and the house. It's so marvelous to be back. And how *clean* everything looks!"

Miriam was amused to find herself as gratified with this last compliment as she was when Barney gave her a rare pat on the back for some meticulously arranged conference or for some particularly diplomatic handling of a difficult client.

It was good to see the family united again, and to see too how much Annie was included in the general reunion. Eileen was genuinely touched at the girl's offer of help while she was on holiday, and when at last the young people went off in her charge, Eileen spoke of her to Miriam.

"She's absolutely splendid with children. We hope she'll be able to take up nursery training. It's what she wants to do, and Lovell and I are going to do all we can to persuade her mother to let her. She's about the most unselfish person I ever met — next to you, I should say."

"Not me!" protested Miriam. "I am *horribly* sel-fish. All I think about is my own affairs."

"Then the virtue's all the greater when you put them aside so readily to come to our aid," said Eileen firmly.

Later that evening when the children were abed and Annie had departed, the three sat by the fire in amicable drowsiness.

"Are you sure you wouldn't sooner be in bed?" asked Miriam.

"No, it's bliss to be here, and honestly I feel better, if anything, than when I went in. The diet's helped a lot, and all I need now is a little exercise to get my legs less wobbly."

"You look more relaxed," agreed Lovell, "but I shouldn't venture out for a day or two. After that hothouse of a hospital you'll find the vicarage garden pretty chilly."

"Pottering round the house will suit me," said Eileen. "And I hope Miriam will stay on now for a holiday instead of being a hard-working house-keeper, and let me look after her for a change."

"I shall stay as long as I'm needed," said Miriam, "but let's see how you feel tomorrow morning before we make plans. I've thoroughly enjoyed myself here. It's been a break — "

"*But*," broke in Eileen, "you have your own affairs to see to, and we've trespassed on your precious free time already. Honestly, my darling Miriam, I am perfectly recovered, and I think next week's check-up will be the last that's needed, so if you want to go ahead with your own plans, *please* feel free."

"Well," said Miriam, weakening in the face of this reasoning, "let's decide tomorrow morning. If all is well, perhaps I could go on Thursday. Now that Annie's here — "

"Even if Annie weren't here we could manage, I feel sure. Lovell can be here pretty well nonstop until Sunday, and the girls are quite big enough to help now."

At that moment the telephone rang and Lovell went to answer it. He returned to say:

"It's for you, Miriam. It's Martin on the telephone."

"Look, Miriam," said Martin, "this Welsh trip has cropped up sooner than I thought. The dealer has some good cattle at the moment, and I propose going down on Saturday and coming back on Sunday. Can we meet?"

Miriam thought quickly.

"What about Sunday lunch with me? Something pretty simple, as I'm in the throes of decorating and the paint may still be wet, but — "

"No, no. I insist on taking you out to lunch. But Sunday will be fine for me. Do you know somewhere?"

"I'll book a table in Caxley," said Miriam. "Shall we say twelve-thirty at 'The Bull'? It's just off the market square."

"Lovely!" said Martin. "Now we've found each other again, it will be good to catch up with old times."

"Yes, indeed," said Miriam politely. But she wished he had said: "Now we've *met* each other again" instead of "*found each other*" which sounded uncomfortably intimate to one of her temperament.

"Martin's coming my way next weekend," she said, returning to the fireside. "And taking me out to lunch."

"Well, he hasn't lost much time," said Lovell, with a satisfaction which his sister found distasteful in the circumstances. But she forbore to retort.

🌿

Next morning, to her surprise, she found that Eileen was in the kitchen before her, and was busy frying bacon and eggs for the family.

She smiled at Miriam's astonishment.

"This is just to show you how fit I am. I feel a positive fraud being treated as an invalid."

"How did you sleep?"

"Like a top. Woke up an hour ago feeling I could mow the lawn, walk to Norwich, and eat a couple of horses."

"Wonderful! You've certainly recovered."

She began to cut bread ready to toast. It was good to see Eileen in command again.

"So, Miriam dear, don't linger here on our behalf if you really want to get back. I couldn't help overhearing your remark to Martin that you were in the midst of decorating. You are an absolute marvel to have dropped everything — paint brushes included — to come all this way."

She put down the fork with which she was turning the bacon and came to put her arms round Miriam.

"This isn't speeding the parting guest. I'd like you to stay, you know, but if you can't now, then come very soon for a real holiday. But if you'd feel happier about getting back, please believe me when I say we can really manage now, and will *never* forget your kindness when we were in trouble."

Miriam hugged her affectionately.

"If you're quite sure, then I might even push off later this morning. The weather seems more settled, and if Annie turns up as usual, I'd feel quite happy about leaving you with that tower of strength."

And so it fell out that at half-past eleven, with her case in the car, sandwiches cut by Eileen, a flask filled by Annie, and a posy of mixed winter flowers collected by the children, Miriam was ready to start on her long journey.

All the family, including Annie, were on the doorstep to wave goodbye. Their embraces had been unusually warm and loving, and Miriam was astonished to realize how sad she felt at parting. To think that just over a week ago she had arrived in a mood of stern duty! Now it was as much as she could do to keep back the tears as she drove away.

"Don't forget you're coming at Easter!" shouted Hazel.

"Before if you can!" added Eileen.

"A thousand thanks!" called Lovell. "I shall be writing."

She hooted all the way down the drive in reply to their valedictions, and had to fumble for a handkerchief when she was safely out of their sight.

The floods were out between St. Neots and Bedford, and traffic was diverted around narrow lanes bordering water-logged fields. At Newport Pagnell there were more floods, but the sky was clear and the wind had dropped to a gentle breeze, and Miriam pushed on steadily.

There was plenty of time now for uninterrupted thought. A lot of good had come from this week's visit. She had learned to know Eileen better, and to appreciate the strength of character that lay behind the babyish good looks. She remembered her gaiety and courage in the face of death at the hospital, her honest gratitude for help given. Now she began to see why Lovell loved her so much. It made her own feelings towards her brother much more comfortable. If Lovell were happy, then she too was happy. It was as simple as that.

And how much greater now was her bond with the children! They were all of them — Lovell, Eileen, and she herself — much closer because of this adversity. She felt better for having gone. It had jolted her out of her own selfish rut, and a good thing too, she told herself.

" 'Cast your bread upon the waters!' " she remembered. Well, she had certainly received a bountiful return.

It was dark when she arrived at Holly Lodge, and Joan was out. Probably having a New Year's Eve drink with friends in Fairacre, thought Miriam, suddenly remembering the date.

She put away the car, and carried her things indoors. The pleasant smell of new paint greeted her. She breathed it in with rapture.

Here she was at last! At home, and alone, ready for all that might befall in the New Year.

What would it hold for her? She remembered Martin, and was warmed by the thought of his friendship which might grow — who knew? — into something dearer.

Well, it was nice to be wanted, Lovell and his family had proved that. But not for always, thought Miriam, looking for a vase for her Norfolk nosegay. She was glad to have met Martin again, glad to know she would see him soon, and glad to know that the bond with her family was more closely knit.

But this was where she was happiest. For her, spinsterhood was truly blessed. She walked into her empty sitting room and closed the door behind her, the better to relish that sweet solitude which to her was the breath of life.

A vision of the vicarage rose before her — the paper chains, the expanding fans and bells, the tinsel, the mistletoe, the holly.

Here there was no holly for Miss Quinn, but she felt a glow as warm as its red berries at the joy of being home, a joy which, she knew, would remain ever green in the years which lay ahead.